Recite - Text copyright © Emmy Ellis 2024
Cover Art by Emmy Ellis @ studioenp.com © 2024

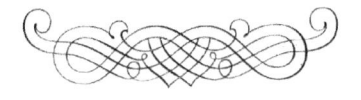

All Rights Reserved

Recite is a work of fiction. All characters, places, and events are from the author's imagination. Any resemblance to persons, living or dead, events or places is purely coincidental.

The author respectfully recognises the use of any and all trademarks.

With the exception of quotes used in reviews, this book may not be reproduced or used in whole or in part by any means existing without written permission from the author.

Warning: The unauthorised reproduction or distribution of this copyrighted work is illegal. No part of this book may be scanned, uploaded, or distributed via the Internet or any other means, electronic or print, without the author's written permission.

RECITE

Emmy Ellis

Chapter One

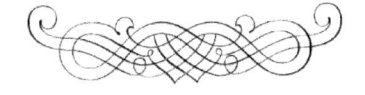

She shouldn't keep coming here, standing at the bungalow window and staring inside.

How many times had she done this now? She'd lost track somewhere around the eleven-visit mark. It had become a compulsion. She'd been told not to come here, but she had anyway — fuck you, Boycie. She'd almost got caught last week, sure the woman in the bed had opened her eyes a touch and seen her, but the target hadn't screamed, like normal people would if someone stood in their back garden in the middle of the night, gawping in at them.

But then…Edna wasn't normal.

Do it, do it, do it…

She had a habit of reciting things—or maybe it wasn't her doing it but a voice inside her head, the one that pushed her to do shit she shouldn't be doing. Like standing here. Precious had wanted to get this over and done with last month, killing Edna and Kayla, but Boycie had put his foot down, telling her to wait. She knew why and in a way agreed: yes, it was best for them to remain under the radar, considering what had happened, and yes, they might be suspected if they stepped in too early to tie up the two loose ends. But the longer those loose ends were alive, the more she worried they'd blab. Both of them knew about the hit on Alice. It could all come back to bite Precious on the arse if she wasn't careful. Now Roach wasn't here to insist Edna and Kayla kept their mouths shut, what was to stop either of them making an anonymous phone call to The Brothers or the police?

In the darkness of three-thirty a.m., she moved back from the window, wishing she was indoors instead, standing over Edna and watching her die, listening for that last breath. Sadly, she turned to leave the garden via the bottom end where a gate led to an alley that went along the backs of the bungalows. She walked quietly, keeping her face covered. She barely saw anyone while out at this time on her little detour on her way home from work, her secret habit.

The idea was to kill Edna by making it look like an overdose, a nice and simple dispatch, although that would mean Precious would have to administer the drugs then sit there and wait for the woman to die. Not that she was complaining, she didn't mind doing it, but what she *did* mind was the worry of leaving a speck of herself behind. If the police didn't agree it was an OD, they'd be on the lookout for whoever had murdered her. Precious' DNA hadn't been recorded anywhere, she'd always been careful not to get arrested, but she'd hate for it to be picked up and filed, just waiting for the day she *did* get caught for something and it was matched to her.

She kept to the edges of the pavements close to the bushes bordering the front gardens. The majority of people would be asleep. Were their lives as complicated as hers? Although saying that, hers wasn't too bad, it was just Edna and Kayla she needed to get rid of, then everything would have gone to plan.

She imagined Boycie in her flat, staying up for her. He'd become her boyfriend of sorts, even though he sometimes slept on the sofa—she liked the bed to herself. It had taken time to adjust, going from Roach to Boycie.

She was using Boycie, she could admit that. And she was *still* using him. There was no way she could end it with him, not when he knew what she'd done. He could get arsey and might go off on one. The twins being involved made matters even more difficult. How was she supposed to ditch Boycie when he could go straight to George and Greg and tell them everything? But maybe she didn't want to ditch him at all. She'd always wanted a partner, children, a proper, stable relationship. Roach hadn't given it to her, and he never would have. Boycie was the type who wanted to settle down, he'd already told her that. So why didn't it feel right? Why did she feel like she wanted to run away? Maybe it'd be okay once she'd killed Edna and Kayla. Maybe the remnants of the past that were still hanging around were preventing her from moving forward and having a happy life.

Maybe she should go back to Edna's right now.

No, she'd do it tomorrow. It'd be safer then. She'd bring weapons to threaten her with, be in disguise, and she'd safeguard herself by using gloves and whatever.

She continued towards home, keeping to the shadows as much as possible. Once she reached her block, she took her balaclava off and shook her hair out. She climbed the steps that led to the balcony outside her flat, popping the key in the lock and stepping inside.

She peered down the hallway to the living room. Boycie wasn't asleep on the sofa, so he must have gone to bed or stayed at his own place. She shrugged and shut the door. Going into the kitchen to toss her keys on the worktop, she stuck the kettle on, needing a cuppa. Then she switched on her phone to see whether Boycie had got hold of her. He had.

BOYCIE: SHALL WE GO CLUBBING WHEN YOU FINISH WORK? THE ROXY'S GOT A TWO-FOR-ONE ENTRY DEAL ON.

Precious shook her head. Yes, at one time she would have gone clubbing straight after work, but lately, she just wanted to come home, have a shower, and go to bed. It was as if Boycie didn't know her anymore, or he'd forgotten she'd changed so much in the past few months. He'd claimed to have loved her for years, but if he truly did, he'd notice she wasn't the same.

Why did she get the feeling men lied to her like she was too stupid to know any different? It really hacked her off.

PRECIOUS: SORRY, JUST GOT BACK. TOO TIRED TO GO CLUBBING. YOU KNOW I DON'T DO THAT CRAP ANYMORE. ARE YOU STAYING AT MINE OR YOURS TONIGHT?

She pressed SEND. A bleep went off.

"Here," he said.

She jumped, turning to look into the hallway. Boycie stood in the doorframe in just his Oddballs boxer shorts covered in neon flowers. She should want to go up to him, to hug him, but she didn't. Part of her resented how he was like Roach, where he thought he could tell her what she could and couldn't do. Even though it made sense to wait to kill Edna and Kayla, it still pissed her off having to do as she was told. Still, they'd first made plans in July, and now it was September. Two months had gone by, so surely the twins wouldn't link their deaths to Alice's and Roach's. Surely Boycie could see now was the time.

"You're late again," he said.

She rolled her eyes. "I didn't realise I had a curfew."

"Did you go to Edna's?"

"Yes. What's that got to do with you?"

"Because I promised you I'd look after you. How can I if you keep nosing in Edna's garden? You're going to get caught one day, you know that, don't you?"

"But I haven't done anything wrong."

"Loitering in the dark on private property is doing something wrong, Presh."

"I suppose so." She wasn't going to argue the toss with him, she couldn't be bothered, and she was still bristling about him mentioning she was late. Who did he think he was?

The kettle had boiled, so she poured water into a cup over a teabag, which reminded her she needed to buy some more at the little Sainsbury's down the road. All the while she made her tea, she sensed Boycie staring at her back. What was he thinking? Did he wonder why he'd agreed to have a relationship with her? Admittedly, she didn't feel the same as she had the night they'd chatted, when she'd confessed what she wanted out of life and he'd done the same. When they'd agreed they were going to grass Roach up to the twins. Her feelings had changed, but she couldn't put her finger on why. Boycie was still the same person, but she'd altered. Maybe seeing Roach being killed was what had done it. Maybe Boycie stepping into his shoes and getting bossy was the reason.

The three of them had been friends for so long she was finding it hard to adjust to life without Roach, even though she'd been the instigator of his death. At the time, it was the only way she could see a clear future where she dictated what she did and Roach didn't. She hadn't factored in that she liked parts of him, the parts that made her laugh until she cried. They'd had some good times, some fun, but he'd become someone she barely knew.

Boycie had told her Roach had been addicted to cocaine, so that explained his personality transplant, but Roach hadn't confided in her that he was a drug user. She'd always thought that he *peddled* drugs, not that he'd taken them. There had been a long list of things he hadn't told her, things she'd been excluded from when Boycie wasn't. They were supposed to be a trio, each of them sharing shit, but it hadn't worked out like that.

Precious hadn't liked being the outcast, so Roach had paid for it.

She'd always been a selfish person, out for what she could get, so it had surprised her that she'd felt bad for Alice. Not at first, not when she'd agreed to kill her, but somewhere along the line, she'd realised Roach had mistreated his ex-wife to such a degree that even Precious didn't find it acceptable. Still, that was in the past now. Alice was dead, so was Roach, and it was time to move on.

"Are you going to stand there and stare at my back like a creepy bastard all night?" She took milk out of the fridge and added a splash to her tea, stirring in one spoonful of sugar. She turned to glare at Boycie.

He walked in to sit at her little table. "No cuppa for me then?"

"Err, you don't get to boss me around anymore. I put up with it when Roach was alive because that's the way things were since we were little, but if you think you can be in a relationship with me and order me about, you've got another think coming."

"Hang on a minute, you're making it sound like I'm a dictator. Christ, all I mentioned was a cup of tea. If it bothers you that much, I'll make it my-fucking-self."

"You do that, and it was the *way* you mentioned it, just so you know for future reference. Like you'd expected me to have made one for you when I made my own. The good girlfriend, always thinking of her fella. Bog off!"

She moved out of the way so he could access the kettle and leaned on the sink unit. This had been her go-to position whenever Roach had been here sitting at the table with Boycie, discussing business. She pushed off the unit, annoyed at old habits dying hard, and walked down the hallway to the living room, parking her arse on the sofa and putting her tea on the table beside her.

Jesus, how bloody boring. Was this the life she'd chosen? No excitement? Was this how it was always going to be, her coming home from work, Boycie there to greet her, expecting her to make the tea? Now she thought about it, he must have taken yet another leaf out of Roach's book because *he'd* always expected her to cook for him. "Make me a steak, Presh. Sort us a sandwich, will you?" If she was going to stay with Boycie, there needed to be a few ground rules put down. If he didn't want to abide by them, he could fuck off.

She considered putting the telly on, but that would just add to her annoyance. A couple sitting together with ITVX on the screen. But wasn't that what she'd wanted? No, it was what she *thought* she'd wanted, and now she had it, she preferred what she'd had with Roach. Casual hookups whenever he felt like it and the rest of the time was her own.

Fucking hell, I'm such a cow. I've led him on, let him think he's going to get a happy ever after.

But she'd have to pretend, just for a while longer. She'd stay with Boycie until the dust settled after Edna's and Kayla's deaths. She'd engineer it so their relationship fizzled out naturally and he was the one who ended it. They'd promise each other they'd keep their secrets, then go their separate ways. With that plan settled in her mind, she smiled at him as he walked into the living room and sat beside her. The scent of coffee wafted over.

"You'll be awake all night with that caffeine," she said. "That's all I need is you tossing and turning in bed while watching crap reels on your phone."

He frowned, acting like a wounded dog. "I'll kip on the sofa then. What's wrong with you anyway? You don't seem the same since Roach died."

"I'm still getting used to the fact that we engineered it all. I didn't think I'd feel guilty, but I do, even if it's only a little bit."

He laughed. "*You*, feel guilty? That's a new one."

"Yeah, well, it surprised me, too." She sipped her tea, scrambling for something else to say before he filled it with questions she didn't want to answer. She opened her mouth too late, and he got in there first.

"What's going on, Precious? You've been weird for a while now, ever since I told you we couldn't kill Edna and Kayla yet. Have you forgotten I know you of old? All your moods, your expressions? You might want to tell your face to keep neutral when you're thinking bad thoughts about me."

"You annoyed me, that's all, ordering me about, but I saw sense in the end. It would be so easy to go inside Edna's. She even leaves her patio doors unlocked some nights. I've worked everything out in my head, and I'd only need to be there for a couple of hours." She ploughed on, determined to show him he wasn't calling the shots anymore. "It's September now, enough time has passed, so I'm going there tomorrow night whether you agree or not. You need to stay here so you're my alibi."

"Then you have to tell me your plan from beginning to end. I'll see if there are any flaws."

That bugged her. "Oh, so you're saying the silly little woman isn't clever enough to work things out by herself? Jesus Christ, you're as bad as Roach sometimes. Did you forget how often I was the one who made solid plans, when you two were sitting here discussing business? Did you forget half the time it was *my* ideas you went with?"

"Sorry, it's just things are different now. You're my girlfriend, so I worry more."

She quite like the sound of that but couldn't understand why she balked at the same time. This was what she'd wanted. This was what she'd dreamed of, and now she had it, she didn't want it anymore. Typical of her. Being in a proper relationship felt constricting. Debilitating. She didn't have any freedom.

"I'm going to be honest," she said, "I'm struggling with *us*, too."

"What do you mean, struggling?"

"Can we pretend we're not in a relationship and we're just still friends who fuck? I find having a name placed on what we are has changed things in my head."

"Yeah, I get what you mean. But I don't want to see anyone else, and I don't want you to either, if that's what you're hinting at."

"No, I'm not interested in anyone else. Anyway, now that's off my chest, I'm off to bed." She couldn't stand to sit there and pick apart what she'd said. Boycie had a bad habit of doing that.

She took her tea into the bedroom, hoping he got the hint and stayed on the sofa tonight. His side of her bed was ruffled where he'd obviously slept while he'd waited for her to get home from work. She sighed, disliking the part of herself that always wanted something more. When she got what she wanted, she needed the next thing, on the next level. If she were honest, she was nothing but trouble for Boycie, and he ought to run as far away from her as he could, the poor bastard.

Chapter Two

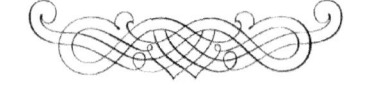

September had rolled around, and Edna's medication had properly kicked in, although if she told anyone what had happened lately, they'd likely say she was having one of her manic, paranoid phases. Hallucinating. But she wasn't. She knew herself well enough to be able to distinguish between paranoia and reality. For a start, her type of paranoia had a dreamlike quality to it, and she viewed things as if they were disjointed scenes clipped together into one TV episode. The person coming to her bedroom window at night and staring inside, that was real, and it wasn't a stuttering visual.

Her reaction to the sighting of someone in a balaclava hadn't been what she'd imagined. She hadn't screamed, she hadn't jumped out of bed to hide or to phone the police. She'd lain there, frozen, half closing her eyes to watch the person. They'd appeared slender, so maybe a teenage boy, and had stayed there for about five minutes—God knew how long they'd been there prior to Edna waking up. Did they know her? Had they watched her tending to her front garden and picked her as their target? Despite her name giving the impression she might be old, she wasn't, so they couldn't have come to do a bit of granny bashing. Then again, if they didn't know who lived here, maybe they'd assumed an old woman did until they'd seen her.

They could have been casing the place, though. Luckily, she didn't have anything worth stealing, unless you counted her telly and ancient laptop, but as a former druggie, she knew how addiction pushed you to nick anything you could get your hands on to fund the habit. Was the person an addict? Lucky for her, when she'd needed drugs, she'd been paid to go to a refuge in disguise—a body suit and mask that made her look like an old woman—so she'd afforded the crap she'd put into her body, but that was all over now. It was time to sort herself out, take her bipolar meds instead of selling them, and try to live some semblance of a normal life.

She'd just about got over the shock that her dealer, Roach, had died. Killed, his head and arm chopped off and left in his dad's back garden. Although his real name was Everett, and he'd sent her to Dolly's Haven to spy on his ex-wife. Edna had known Alice would be killed, yet she'd gone ahead and obeyed Roach anyway. If he wasn't dead, she'd have convinced herself that the peeping Tom was something to do with him.

"But it still could be," she whispered, wishing someone was there to hear what she'd said so they could respond and tell her everything would be all right.

Roach had friends. Maybe they were worried Edna wouldn't keep her mouth shut about being a mole at Haven. Maybe the peeper had been sent to get rid of her, only they hadn't had the guts to go through with it. Yet.

"Stop inventing things that aren't even true."

She sat at her little desk in the living room. Today's tasks were to do some online questionnaires and surveys, which she got paid for, then go and have lunch at the Noodle, and after that, she'd do a bit of weeding out the front. She'd found if she had a plan for each day, she could cope better.

Maybe she should get hold of Kayla. Or Vicky, as she'd been known. Find out if anyone was watching her, too.

She'd told herself to stop contacting Kayla — any link to her was a bad one, considering she'd lured Alice to Curls and Tongs where the murder had taken place. All Edna had done was listen in at Haven, she hadn't had a big role in actually *killing* the woman, but hmm, being linked to Kayla wasn't such a good idea. Not when everything had now died down. According to the papers, the police thought Roach's death was tied to Alice's — one person out to destroy them both. But that wasn't true, not that Edna would tell anyone that. She had a horrible feeling the twins had dealt with Roach after finding out he'd arranged a hit on Alice.

Edna itched to text Kayla so deleted the woman's number. She told herself to mind her own business now, to never get involved with anyone from the drug scene, and to try and straighten her life out.

Maybe she should think about getting a job. Then again, doing the surveys on the side added to her benefits, and she still had the money Roach had paid her, tucked away nicely in a shoebox under her bed. Perhaps that's what the peeper was after. Money, jewellery. He might have assumed, because she lived in a bungalow, left to her by her late nan, that she was a vulnerable resident easily overpowered if he broke in.

Instead of opening the first survey email, she browsed a cheap gadget site and bought a CCTV camera, twenty quid. She could download the app that went with it and pay a small subscription so it recorded, played back footage, and also stored it in the cloud. She'd point it towards her bedroom window, keep one curtain open each night, and see how often the weirdo came back, if they even did. At least then, if something bad happened to her, there'd be a record of it.

Edna got on with a few surveys, mainly for washing powder, fabric softener, and bleach. She wasn't particularly interested in any of it, so maybe she shouldn't have clicked the Household Goods icon. Still, she did her best, giving answers as if she were an enthusiastic housewife, which the text had rudely stated this was aimed at, then she moved on to the cooking section. As she'd been a chef at Haven and she enjoyed cooking, she found these surveys more interesting. Before she knew it, three hours had passed by and it was time for lunch. She closed her laptop down and found her red baseball cap, slapped it on, and left the bungalow.

She kept her head down as she passed the home opposite. A while back, she'd had a row with the nosy cow who lived there. When the twins had last been here, they'd gone over to have a word with Nose Ache. Edna would bet they'd asked the old woman to keep an eye on her. Well, there was nothing for her to see or report on, unless she wanted to tell them how often Edna did her front garden, or how a couple of times a week she walked to the Noodle for lunch, not that

Nosy would know where she'd gone unless she followed her. But having lunch wasn't a crime. Anyway, Nessa, the manager there, had probably told the twins Edna had become a regular. She likely had to report things like that.

It didn't take long to get to the pub. She pushed open the door and went straight up to the bar, ordering a coffee that she'd pour from the self-serve machine. Plus a tuna baguette and a packet of cheese and onion crisps. She paid and sat at her usual table, taking her phone out and opening the survey app. She may as well earn another tenner while she was at it.

Her food arrived halfway through the survey, so she paused it to eat. There had been a time when she'd considered asking Roach to help her fund a new baking business, cakes, but as she had no qualifications in catering, she wasn't sure how she'd be able to do that. Still, she'd ask Nessa now if there was any chance she could bake cupcakes and muffins to be sold in the pub, although she suspected the answer would be no. There were likely rules and regulations she had to follow, health and safety, all that shit.

Edna carried her plate to the bar and smiled at Nessa. "Have you ever thought about selling cakes for people to have with their coffee?"

Nessa shook her head. "Not really, no."

"Oh, it's just that I'm good at baking and wondered if you'd be interested in sampling some of my cakes. To be honest, I'm trying to sort my life out, you know, get a job and whatever, but it's hard. People don't want the likes of me with no qualifications. I used to take drugs, and nobody wants to give me a chance."

Nessa seemed to soften at that. Was she one of those bleeding heart types? "Why don't you come here tomorrow and do some baking in our kitchen, at least then it's in a hygienic place. Not saying that your kitchen isn't, but you know what I mean."

"Yeah, I get what you're saying." Edna couldn't believe she might well have an opening for a job. Why hadn't she asked about this before now?

Because you needed to get your head sorted, that's why.

As she'd been selling her bipolar prescription to Roach, plus sniffing cocaine instead, she'd been a bit of a mess, easily manipulated into going to Haven in that stupid disguise and pretending to be an old lady. Was that why he'd persuaded her to sell him the pills, and he'd offered her the white stuff, because he knew she'd become addicted and rely on him? His offer of a good wage while she'd worked at Haven had meant she'd have agreed to anything.

Manipulative bastard.

What if Nessa offered her a job and Edna had to work here every day? It would get her out of the house and feel as though she was living again instead of struggling through treacle.

"What time shall I come?"

"Let's say ten, so the breakfast rush is done and dusted, then you won't get in the chef's way too much."

"Okay, thank you. I'll see you then."

Edna went back to her table to collect her coffee cup. She poured the free refill and sat again, thinking about all the possibilities that could be waiting in her future. Wages. Some permanence. People raving about her cakes like they had at Haven. Dare she dream that a better life was just around the corner?

Chapter Three

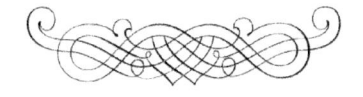

Precious had had a sore tummy since last night. She didn't get scared often, but she was starting school today. Some of the big kids would be there, ones she'd called names and screeched at down the park. They'd probably pick on her at playtime to get her back because she wouldn't have Mummy to shoo them off. She said if you played with fire you got burnt, but

Precious didn't like fire, so she didn't know what that was all about. What if they punched her? Would the teachers tell them off? Maybe she should stop shouting nasty names at people, then she wouldn't get in so much trouble. She wouldn't have them coming after her. Once, one of them waited behind a tree at the park and jumped out when she went past, tripping her over. She'd grazed her knees and everything, and Mummy cleaned them with TCP, and it hurt a lot.

Daddy said she was his little fighter and he was proud that she stuck up for herself. She was like the boy he'd never had.

"Is it like playgroup?" she asked, walking down the street with Mummy.

A lot of her playgroup friends wouldn't be in her new class; they were going to the other school. Mummy said that was okay, she'd soon make new ones. She'd also said to Daddy, when she thought Precious wasn't there, that those "poor kids" were probably really happy they weren't going to the same school because now Precious couldn't bully them.

She clutched Mummy's hand harder. What if nobody liked her? What if they called her mean names like she did to that little cow down the street? What if they were as horrible as she was?

The school came into view around the corner. She'd been there for a visit last month, and the secretary had shown them round. It was big with lots of corridors, and she'd get lost. The dinner hall stretched on forever, monkey bars at the end against the wall because it was also used for PE. There was a cupboard full of balls and little bean bags to teach you to catch and throw. Precious knew how to do that already, Daddy had taught her.

Butterflies danced in her chest. That's what Mummy said the fluttering was anyway, but Precious didn't know how they got inside her. Did they fly in her mouth while she slept? The only other time they came was just before she picked on someone or Father Christmas was coming.

"You're going to have a lovely day, all right?" Mummy said. "All this worry will go as soon as you get in there."

She guided her across the playground, weaving around clusters of other mums all having a chinwag, then they headed towards an open door. A lady stood there, letting all the children in, and Precious remembered her from the day she'd come here for the visit. Miss Taylor.

"Hello," Miss Taylor said. "How are you today, Precious?"

She was all right now she'd seen the teacher. She liked her. "Okay."

Mummy kissed her on the cheek and said she'd see her later at three o'clock; she'd sounded funny when she'd said that, her voice all wobbly. Three o'clock seemed such a long way away, and Precious wanted to cry. It got her angry. Daddy said only babies cried.

She watched Mummy walk across the playground, and her eyes stung so much she blinked a lot. Miss Taylor gently moved her out of the doorway and told her to go into the cloakroom, but Precious sidled along and stared out of the window. Mummy paused at the gate and turned. She seemed shocked and upset to find Precious staring at her, and she lifted her hand to cover her mouth. Did she want to cry, too?

"Give her a big wave," Miss Taylor said brightly, "and smile, otherwise she's going to worry you're unhappy."

Precious wasn't unhappy, not anymore. Miss Taylor's hand on her shoulder made her feel better. So she did what the teacher had said. Mummy smiled so big and waved back, then she walked off down the lane towards home.

Precious went into the cloakroom and found her peg. It had a picture of a bumble bee and her name underneath it. She remembered it from her visit—Miss

Taylor had told her to keep it in her head so she'd know where to put her things, so she'd recited "bee, bee, bee" for ages and ages.

She hung her bag up and slid her shoes underneath the bench, taking her plimsolls out of her bag and struggling to put them on. Miss Taylor crouched to help her.

"She helped me, too," a little boy beside her said. "The stupid elastic's too tight on them. My mum said I'm not big enough to have laces yet, but I want laces so I'm going to learn how to do them."

"It'll soon loosen up." Miss Taylor stood. "Come on, everybody, off you go into story corner. It's time to take the register."

Precious didn't know what that was. She hung her coat up over her bag and followed everybody to a large square of carpet. The boy sat next to her.

"What's your name?" he whispered.

"Precious," she said.

"I'm Everett, and that's Boycie."

"That's a stupid name."

"No one ever calls him by his proper one. Even Miss Taylor calls him Boycie because he won't answer her if she doesn't."

Boycie shuffled over on his bum. One of his front teeth was missing. He stared at her. "You live at the other end of my street."

Precious shrugged. She hadn't seen him before. "Dunno. I'm only allowed to play down my end." That was true, but she didn't listen to Mummy and sometimes ran up there to cause trouble.

"I've seen you," he said. "You're always with that girl with the ginger hair."

"That's my next-door neighbour. She's got a ginger brother an' all who picks his nose and stuff."

The boys flopped around in laughter.

Miss Taylor clapped and sat on a chair in front of the class. "Quiet, please."

She took the register, which was calling out names and everyone saying they were here. Then she sent them to tables, and they chanted numbers from one to a hundred. Precious recited them in her head afterwards when it was milk time because she wanted to be the best at remembering. They sipped from little square cartons through a straw, and Miss Taylor gave them a slice of apple each. Then it was time to go out to play. Precious ran around with Everett and Boycie, giggling her head off whenever they tried to tag her.

She reckoned she might like them.

By the end of the day, her tummy had stopped hurting. School wasn't that bad after all, especially because she had dinners and today was sausage and chips, and for pudding a cake with sprinkles on top.

Mummy stood in the playground waiting for her. Precious skipped up to her and held out a drawing she'd done this afternoon.

"Is that for me?" Mummy asked

"Miss Taylor said you can put it on the fridge, but she wants to talk to you about it in the morning."

Mummy looked at the picture and frowned, then smiled like she did whenever she pretended everything was all right. Was the picture bad? It was of Precious standing over the little cow down the road, a knife in her hand.

Mummy paled. "Was school good?"

"Yeah. I made friends with two boys. One of them is over there, look." Precious pointed towards Boycie.

"Oh, he lives in our street."

"That's what he said. He's nice to me, he is."

"Then you be nice back."

Why did Mummy have to say that and spoil things when today had turned into such a happy day? Yes, Precious was nasty to the children in their street. Mums always came to the front door and shouted, their kids sobbing. Mummy told her she shouldn't be mean, but something in Precious' head told her to do it anyway. She didn't understand why she didn't do as she was told, just that she liked seeing other children cry. Daddy reckoned she was a bruiser.

Pretending Mummy hadn't upset her, she waved at Boycie and left the playground.

"Shepherd's pie and peas tonight," Mummy said.

"I had sausage and chips for lunch and a bit of cake."

"You'll go pop if you eat any more." Mummy laughed.

Precious liked it when Mummy laughed.

So why do I do things that make her cry?

She didn't understand that either. Maybe she was like Mrs Courson three doors down had said: "You're the Devil's child, you little bitch. Fuck off home and stay away from my house. You'll turn into nothing but trouble when you're older, you mark my words."

Precious had given her the middle finger, like Daddy sometimes did to people down the pub when he'd had too much lager, then she'd run home and waited for the woman to come knocking. She hadn't, so Precious had been rude to her the next day, too. She'd stomped to their house that time, saying Precious needed a good smack.

"You can play out before dinner, but you have to be a good girl," Mummy said. "Please be a good girl, Precious, okay? Let's have one evening where the doorbell doesn't ring, yes?"

"I promise to be good."

Although she should never promise that. She was already thinking of who she could slap.

Chapter Four

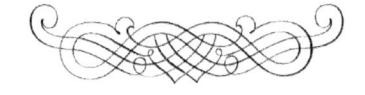

The Widow didn't think it was too bad working for the twins. They left her alone like Roach had. Well, not at first, but once they'd realised she was quite capable of running the Orange Lantern by herself, thank you very much, they'd been willing to step back. Good job, too, because she didn't like people standing there looking over her shoulder, watching every move she made. It irritated the shit out of her.

She wasn't sure about the newest woman who called herself Goddess. Yes, she certainly looked like one and pulled in a lot of new punters, but Widow had a feeling there was more to her than met the eye. She'd held back from saying anything so far because it might look like she was jealous, but that wasn't the case. It was because Precious had been the one to take Goddess on when she'd applied for the job, apparently hearing of the opening via word of mouth, and Widow hadn't wanted to undermine Precious' decision. Now she came to think about it…what word? What mouth? Who the hell had Goddess heard about the job from?

That was a mistake on Widow's part, to not have checked, probably because Precious had always been very good at sussing people out and she hadn't steered Widow wrong so far. Still, there was always a first time to fuck up, wasn't there, and this might well be it. But without any proof that Goddess was there for reasons other than selling her body, there wasn't a lot she do could do but watch her. *Widow* had taken this job for other reasons, so she knew damn well it was possible Goddess could have. Widow hadn't come here with the desire to run the Orange Lantern but to kill Roach—but someone had got there first. She'd dithered, taken too long to get the courage up to do it. She'd had her reasons for wanting rid of him, ones she wouldn't think about today, not when it would sour her mood.

Maybe she should tell the twins of her suspicions regarding Goddess. Would they believe what amounted to a sixth sense, though? Would they want proof of any wrongdoing? Widow didn't have any, and she'd been observing Goddess for ages now. Having heard the rumours about The Brothers and seeing them here when they'd first taken over the brothel, she could well imagine how angry they'd be if she didn't open her mouth and kept everything to herself, even if the only issue was that Goddess had a strange *air* about her. What harm would it do to tell them anyway? If she was wrong, she was wrong, but if she was right, it was evidence that she should always follow her gut.

She sighed and reached for the phone on her desk in the office. Pressed the icon for the twins and held the phone to her ear. The ringing sounded urgent, faster than normal, but it must be her perception. She put it down to worry that they'd shout at her for bringing them such a stupid problem to deal with, which likely wasn't even a problem in the first place.

The ringing stopped. "All right, Widow."

She recognised the voice as George's. Those two might look the same, but their tones were slightly different.

"What's up?" he asked.

"That new woman, Goddess. There's something about her that's bothering me. I couldn't tell you what it is, and she hasn't done anything wrong that I'm aware of, but I'm just getting a feeling about her and have done since day dot."

"Like a vibe," George said. "I know what you mean. How come you're only just telling us about it now?"

"Because I've got nothing concrete. I've been a tad uneasy from the start, but with Roach dying and the brothel changing hands, I put it on the back burner... Don't get me wrong, she's nice enough, and she does her job well, but there's something about her that's off. I don't know whether it's because she thinks she's superior to everyone else, but whatever it is, she doesn't quite fit. I haven't said anything to Precious about it because she was the one who took her on. And Precious tends to get a bit, well, *precious* about things if you go against her decisions."

"Do you want us to come down and have a word with Goddess?" George asked.

"If you can make out it's normal procedure, that you need to check whether she's settled in or not, then that would be better than outright saying someone's grassed her up for being odd. I don't want her to know I'm watching her."

"Fair enough, we can do that. What time's she next in?"

"She's got a daytime shift. This afternoon starting at two until six, then she's back from ten until two."

"Right then, we'll come now."

The line went dead. Widow stared at the phone. Maybe she was stupid to expect him to say goodbye, but then this was George she was talking about here. She placed the receiver in the dock and left the office, bumping into Jessica, one of the women who preferred to work days. She had children so chose half nine until half two. Blonde, skinny, and pretty, she drew in the type of punter who liked the schoolgirl look, hence why she had a short, pleated black skirt on, a white blouse, and a stripy tie. Her hair, in side pigtails, and brown kohl freckles on her cheeks finished off the illusion. Widow had often wondered whether Jessica felt slightly gross pretending to be a schoolgirl when she had children herself.

"Oh, sorry," Jessica said. "Didn't mean to wallop into you there. I was just coming to tell you that Goddess said she's not going to be in today."

That annoyed Widow, and she fought to retain her composure. "Why did she get hold of you and not me?"

Jessica shrugged. "God knows, she just sent me a text message. I thought it was a bit rude to be fair, not only using me as her messenger but not going to you direct. Maybe she's scared of you."

"Right, well, thanks for telling me. I'll just give her a ring now."

Widow stomped into her office, picking up the phone to ring the twins again, not Goddess. She didn't trust herself not to have a go at the woman. Goddess knew the rules. She *knew* who had to be spoken to.

I don't need shit going on at work when I've got it in my private life.

Widow prodded the icon to connect the line. George picked up straight away, laughing and saying she was impatient and they'd be there in a minute

"Calm your tits."

"My tits wouldn't ordinarily be upset, but Jessica's just come up to me and said Goddess won't be in today. Now one, it's pissed me off because it's put me in a right bind: I've got to find someone else to fill her slots quickly. And two, she told Jessica about it and not me. I'll not stand for that. *I'm* the one who runs the Lantern, not Jessica. I'm not saying it's Jessica's fault, she was good and came and told me what was going on, but for fuck's sake. Maybe this is why Goddess has got under my skin. Maybe it's because she thinks she's the boss or she can do what the fuck she likes. Well, she'll soon learn she can't."

"What's her address?" George asked.

Widow checked her file and gave it to him. "What are you going to do, go round there and ask her why she hasn't come to work?"

"I don't see why not, seeing as we're her employers. If she didn't give Jessica a reason for not being there, then we're within our rights to go around and ask. Even if we're not, we'll do it anyway. If she's ill then she should have fucking said so. Don't worry, we'll deal with it."

Once again, the line went dead. Widow propped the receiver back in the dock. Not once had she known of a woman who hadn't followed all the rules at work. It was clear Goddess had a hymn sheet of her own she sang to and wasn't interested in being part of a choir. If Widow had her way, she'd tell Goddess she was no longer welcome here, but she had a feeling that due to the money she brought in, the twins would want to keep her on. Roach would have. She thought about him a lot. Who he'd shown her he was compared to the reality that, underneath his Roach persona, he was a man called Everett who'd lived a suburban life. She'd never have guessed he was two people. He'd become her target as Roach, the man who sold drugs to—

Don't think about home life at work!

"Maybe that's why I've picked up on something with Goddess," she muttered. "Maybe I never want to be duped by someone again so I've been more alert, watching her."

She sighed and scanned the roster to check who had a day off today. She phoned Amanda first to see if she'd come and cover Goddess' lunchtime shift. She said yes, she could do with the extra money, and also offered to work tonight. Widow agreed. With that dilemma sorted, she left the office and went to the kitchen, standing beside Jessica and sticking the kettle on.

"I forgot to ask," Widow said, thinking it best she double-checked, "did Goddess say why she couldn't come to work?"

"No. I'll show you the text if you like." Jessica took her phone out of her pocket and found the message, turning the screen Widow's way.

GODDESS: CAN YOU TELL WIDOW I WON'T BE AT WORK TODAY FOR EITHER OF MY SHIFTS.

"That's not on, is it?" Jessica said. "She didn't even say please and thanks. I mean, we all know the rules and she signed an agreement saying she'd abide by them. I don't even know why she picked me, it's not like we're friends or anything."

"Where did she get your number from then?"

"Oh, she asked for everyone's." Jessica frowned. "And now I'm wondering if that's a bit odd."

Widow pondered that. Maybe Goddess had wanted to make friends with her colleagues, hence asking for their numbers. But... "When was this?"

"When she first started."

"Has she messaged you before today?"

"No."

"Not being funny, but it's not as if she wants to be buddy-buddy then, is it? If that was the case, she'd have messaged you way before now. Thanks for letting me know about that. I'll go and question some of the others. If Goddess gets hold of you again, don't respond, and let me know straight away."

Widow left the kitchen. She'd have a cup of tea later, but first she needed to do a bit of detective work. On the jamb of each bedroom door were small indicator panels with either green or red lights lit. Green indicated the women were free. Widow tapped on all the green doors in turn. Each lady stated they'd given Goddess their number but hadn't interacted with her via messages or calls. Widow thanked them and went downstairs to the office. She phoned George again and explained what she'd discovered.

"That sounds pretty suss to me," she said. "Ask for phone numbers and not use them? Why make out you wanted the numbers to be friends but then do fuck all about it? I'm now getting worried she's been sent to spy on us either by another leader or... Fuck. What if it's the Old Bill?"

"Jesus. Right, we're just pulling up to her house now," George said. "We'll get the truth out of her. If she suddenly feels a lot better and decides to come into work, I'll let you know."

"I've already sorted her replacement now, though."

"Okay, we'll get back to you after we've spoken to her. If she's not in, we'll send someone to watch her place, watch *her* for the foreseeable."

Widow got a goodbye in before he had a chance to end the call. She returned to the kitchen to finally make her tea. Her earlier mention of the police sending Goddess here gave her pause. There would be direct proof that this wasn't just a massage parlour. Maybe Goddess had taken photos and even videos to prove what went on. Or maybe this was all in Widow's imagination. She'd like to think it wasn't, because who wanted to admit they'd got something so wrong? But she'd bet her last quid Goddess was up to no good. Hopefully the twins would work out what it was.

Chapter Five

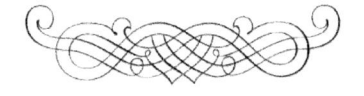

George had mixed feelings about going to see Goddess. When he'd first set eyes on her just after they'd taken over the Orange Lantern, he'd sensed a vibe about her, too, although it wasn't anything like Widow must have felt. He'd fancied her, plain and simple, and it bothered him because he didn't want anything to do with women. Greg had Ineke in his life, and she was proving to be a pest, so why the fuck would George want the same? Sadly, Ineke seemed to like stirring the pot, trying to cause trouble in George and Greg's relationship. What she didn't understand was that Greg had spotted it and was taking notes on her behaviour. It wouldn't be long before he told her a few home truths, the type where he didn't hold back.

The thing with Ineke was they were worried about her state of mind and how she'd respond to their usual brand of telling it like it is. She'd been treated appallingly by her mother, indifferently by her father, and her move from Amsterdam to London had been a fresh start. However, despite her having problems, it didn't mean she could get away with creating them for George and Greg. She had to understand they were twins, they had a special bond, and nothing she could do would break that. Much as she'd tried to be the only one in Greg's life, she'd realised she'd always come second. She'd been fine with that at first but had soon changed her tune.

George pushed her from his mind, otherwise he'd get himself in a bad mood. He parked outside Goddess' place and gave the outside the once-over. It stood in a row of narrow detached houses, all of them white with black-framed windows. They looked like they cost a small fortune. No hedges or fences around the front lawns, and gravel paths bisected each garden and led to tall wooden gates between each property. It had a cookie cutter feel to it, everything the same apart from the cars parked at the kerbs.

"Fuck me, talk about a visually boring place to live," George said.

"Maybe there's comfort in everything being the same." Greg stared out of the window. "I really feel that 'same' can be a good thing. I just wish Ineke would try to understand that I don't want so much change in my life. She hasn't mentioned kids again, though, thank God."

"I was just thinking about her as it happens," George said. "But I stopped myself else I'd get pissed off. I used to think she was a really nice girl, but the more you tell me about her, the more I think she's got mental health issues that need to be dealt with—they're ingrained, like her mother's. I don't feel she's in the right headspace to be in a relationship at the moment, not after what she suffered in Amsterdam."

"Yep, she's needy more than what she said she would be. I don't think she realised what a relationship with me would be like. I can't devote all my time to her, and that's what she deserves. I don't know how I'm going to tell her, though, without her going off the rails and feeling abandoned. I've tried to love her, but it's still just a strong like. I think I was just caught up in her vulnerability when I first met her. I let being the knight in shining armour sweep me away while I swept *her* away."

"Fucking hell, I didn't expect you to go deep, but at least it means you're opening up. So do I take it you're going to end things with her at some point?"

"Yeah, I just don't know when."

Greg opened the driver's-side door and left the taxi. He stood on the pavement, glancing at all the mirror-image houses. Maybe he was wishing their life was the same as it had been before Ineke had come along. Maybe that's what his comment had meant. George felt for him, because he'd honestly thought Greg had met his soul mate. But it just went to show that attraction disguised itself as potential love sometimes.

Once again, George pushed her out of his mind. He walked up Goddess' garden path, checking to see if anyone watched from inside or whether there were hidden cameras that the average person wouldn't clock. He didn't spot any, but that didn't mean there was nothing there. He pressed the bell and waited. The glass in the door was clear and gave him good view of wooden stairs directly ahead. To the right, a slender hallway with two doors. One at the end was the kitchen, a sink unit visible. It seemed like the house was empty. It had that air about it when no one was at home.

He rang the bell again, then called through the letterbox, "Are you in, love?"

With no response, he moved to the gate and turned the ring handle. It opened, and he strode down the passage into a rear garden completely covered in white gravel. A three-arm rotary washing line stood in the centre, a few clothes flapping in a slight breeze. So she'd either been here this morning and hung the washing out or it was one of yesterday's jobs that hadn't been completed. He walked towards it and touched the arm of a long-sleeved T-shirt. It was still damp, and as it hadn't rained for a few days, it confirmed she'd been home this morning.

He left the garden and joined Greg out the front. He happened to be talking to who George assumed was a neighbour. The brunette woman held the handle of a pushchair, the baby boy inside smacking a rattle against his leg and squealing. He gave George a toothless smile, then shoved the rattle in his mouth and rubbed his gums on it.

"So she was here this morning?" Greg asked.

The woman nodded. "Yes, I saw her getting into the back of a dark-grey SUV. The driver was a black bloke and the passenger was a white woman with long, frizzy ginger hair."

"Had you seen them before?" Greg asked.

"No."

"Did she come out of the house and just get in the car or did they go to her front door?"

"She came out as if she'd been expecting them. Maybe they've gone for lunch, I don't know."

"What time was this?" George asked. "Because it looks like you've been out." He gestured to a couple of shopping bags in the basket under the pram.

"I nipped to the little shop, yes. The SUV came about ten. I know it was that time because that's when I give the baby his snack. Half a banana today." She smiled, seeming pleased she could speak to someone.

George felt a bit sorry for her. "Are you lonely by any chance?"

"Sometimes," she said.

"Do you need a job?"

"No, I'm still on maternity leave. I'll be fine once I get back into the office. I can actually have adult conversations all day, then."

"I don't want to sound rude, but are you a single mother?"

"What's that got to do with anything?" she asked.

"Because we like to help people, that's all, so if you're struggling…" George smiled at her and took a business card out of his jacket pocket, plus one of his envelopes containing fifty quid. He handed both over. "Don't take offence, but buy yourself something nice. And if you ever need a job, give us a bell."

"Oh, right, thank you," she said. "And if you must know, my husband died when I was six months pregnant."

"Oh fuck, sorry to hear that. I didn't mean to put my foot in it."

"It's fine. I get used to it more every day. Although it isn't fine, not really. Is there anything else, because I need to get him inside for his lunch." She flapped a hand at the buggy. "Then we're off to the park."

Greg thanked her for her time, and they got in the taxi.

"What did you make of that, then?" George asked. "Goddess obviously knew the people she was going with."

"It's not like it's something unheard of, though, bruv. People *do* have friends and they *do* happen to go out."

George didn't appreciate the sarcasm. "Very fucking funny, but you knew exactly what I meant."

"So she ditched work to go out with her mates."

"But what if they're not her friends? What if they *are* the Old Bill like Widow said—they're colleagues? We've bought the fucking house. It's now a brothel. Yes, we told Widow we didn't want anything to do with it if she ever got caught for running a sex den, and as far as we're concerned, she pays us rent and bills combined, and she uses the house at her own discretion, but what if the courts don't see it that way? What if they believe we knew what she was doing there all along? What if, under pressure, some of the women tell the police we're their employers?"

"But why would the police even be looking at the Orange Lantern? Unless a copper went there for sex or someone told them about it, how would they even know it exists? Having said that, I'm glad you're looking at all options, but on this occasion, I really do think we're worrying over nothing. She chose to work at the Lantern. She decided to have a day off. All right, it's not ideal that she's put Widow in the shit by not doing her shifts, but she knows damn well one of the other women will take over for her. The only bit we should be annoyed about is the fact that she spoke to Jessica and not Widow. Now that needs to be stamped out. Goddess can't just do whatever she likes willy-nilly. She's got people to answer to—and that's us *and* Widow."

"Hang on a sec..."

George got out of the taxi and went up the brunette woman's garden path. Again, clear glass in the front door, and he spotted the buggy parked at the bottom of the stairs. He tapped on the doorframe. She poked her head around the kitchen door, then walked up the hallway towards him and opened up.

"Sorry to bother you again, but did you happen to see the number plate of the SUV?"

"I did, it was a vanity one. L, 1, T, 3."

"Cheers for that." George left her to it and got back in the taxi. "She remembered the number plate, so I'll just send it to Colin."

DS Colin Broadley had become their new police officer on the inside. Janine, the old one, had put it to him that he could acquire justice in different ways to how he did it in his job. When Colin's wife had been raped and murdered in their own home, he'd gone off the rails, his moral compass skewing. The tragedy had changed his mindset. Before, he'd been a by-the-book copper, but now he wanted people caught and dealt with no matter what.

George found Colin's name in the contact list of their work burner. They'd given Colin a burner, too.

GG: CAN YOU RUN A CHECK ON A NUMBER PLATE FOR ME? L, 1, T, 3.

Colin didn't reply straight away, so he was either out on a job or busy accessing the police system. Janine used to make out, if any of her searches were flagged, that she'd seen the driver of said number plate driving erratically or some such thing to cover for why she'd looked it up. She'd talked Colin through how to do certain things, so George assumed the man would do the same as her.

COLIN: IT BELONGS TO JOSEPH BAINS. 43 SHEPHERD'S ROAD. MARRIED TO A FARAH BAINS. NO CHILDREN.

GG: CHEERS.

George repeated the information to his brother.

"So she's pals with a married couple," Greg said. "Big deal. Ask Colin if he can find any link between Goddess and this Farah. For all we know, they could be sisters."

George racked his brain to remember Goddess' real name.

GG: ANY LINKS WITH A DANIKA COUSINS?

COLIN: GIVE ME A FEW MINUTES FOR THAT ONE. NIGEL'S JUST WALKED IN.

Nigel was Colin's senior officer, an apparent pain up the arse.

"Should I get hold of Bennett to check CCTV?" George asked Greg.

"Yeah, because then we might get a direction the SUV went in, even if we don't get the final destination."

George got on with that, receiving a reply from Colin not long after he'd sent a text to Bennett. Danika Cousins didn't appear to have any links to Farah Bains nor Farah's maiden name.

"No links on file," he said to Greg, "but that doesn't mean anything."

The phone rang, Bennett's name on the screen. George put it on speaker.

"All right, mate?" George asked.

"Not too bad, ta. About that car. It's currently parked outside one of the warehouses down the road where yours is. I've got the camera on it now. No one's inside the vehicle, but I checked the previous recording, and three people entered the warehouse. The one you need is two doors down from yours with the red double doors. I did a Google, and it belongs to a Mr Joseph Bains. Does that ring any bells?"

"Yeah. Thanks for your help. Someone will drop an envelope round later."

"Cheers. Let me know if you need this camera switched off at any point."

George had gone spare last month when Bennett had warned him a new camera had gone up. They didn't need their warehouse to torture people anymore, not now they had the cottage in the woods, but it was still annoying that the option had been taken away from them—unless they asked Bennett to make the CCTV go offline for however long it needed to be out of action. The problem was, with the amount of times they killed people, the camera would be switched off too much and would become a red flag.

"Will do." George ended the call and turned to Greg. "What do you think?"

"She's friends with people who run a business that needs a warehouse. That's not exactly illegal, is it?"

"But the reason Widow phoned us is because Goddess has been acting odd. We need to find more about this Joseph character before we move forward. We won't bother Colin with it, we'll ask our usual suspects if they've heard anything about him. We'll send some of our men out to question others, too. I'd rather not let this trio know we're watching them until we have any evidence that proves they're up to no good. For all we know, Goddess may just be giving off some kind of vibe and she's not a bad person. Maybe she's new to the game and is finding her feet."

Greg rubbed a hand over his mouth. "That's not right, because she said she worked for an escort agency before and the reason she left that job was because she actually liked having sex with the clients. The agency didn't allow any of that to go on. If you remember, she admitted to Precious she needs sex in order to feel wanted."

"She'd be better off in a relationship with someone then," George said.

"Hmm, but I'm starting to see the benefits of having no-strings-attached sex and being able to walk away from the person afterwards. No burdens, no hassles."

Fuck me, he really has had enough of Ineke. "Okay, let's go and speak to some of our nosy bastards out on the streets. But first, we'll go by the Bains' house. I just want to get a feel for them, who they are, before we jump in with both feet."

"What was their address again?"

"Forty-three Shepherd's Road."

"Right."

Greg set off, driving sedately. George wanted to tell him to get a fucking move on but decided to keep his mouth shut. Instead, he took a lemon sherbet from the glove box and shoved it in his mouth to stop him from talking, something he did often.

His mind entertained a million scenarios about Goddess, none of them good. While he remembered, he sent Will a message to go to Goddess' place and watch for when she got home, then he could follow her if she left the house later on. George made a point that he wanted eyes on her at all times. When Will went off shift at midnight, someone else would come to take his place.

George had wondered whether this was madness on their part to be listening to the intuition of someone they barely knew, but as he'd done in the past himself, he'd ignored many gut feelings and things had gone tits up. If Widow had worried enough that she'd contacted them, then there must be something wrong.

However it turned out, it was best to get it looked into.

He'd rather be safe than sorry.

Chapter Six

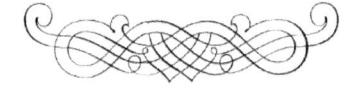

Precious had been at school for two years now. In September, she'd have a new teacher, Mrs Watson. She wasn't too keen on her, but never mind. Like Mummy said, you couldn't have it all your own way, could you. It didn't stop Precious from wanting it, though, and being annoyed when she didn't get it.

She sighed — she'd been naughty again and didn't like being stared at by Miss Taylor. When she upset her, she always wished she hadn't. Her teacher was the one person she didn't want to disappoint, yet she had, even though she'd tried so hard not to. Something inside her pushed her to be naughty, and while she knew it was happening and she should stop it, she didn't want to, no matter the consequences. It didn't help that Everett had egged her on this time, although she didn't see him *being told off. He always seemed to get away with it.*

"Why did you take Samuel's sandwich from his lunch box and put it in the bin?" Miss Taylor asked.

"I don't know."

Precious was usually proud of what she'd done, but today it felt different. Everett had said she should fib, especially because he'd told her to nick the sandwich. He didn't like Samuel, said he was stinky and dirty because his Mummy didn't wash his clothes. He did smell of cheese, but Precious thought that was because he liked Wotsits.

Miss Taylor had sent everyone out to morning play, keeping Precious behind. "Samuel doesn't have any lunch now, all he had was that sandwich. How do you feel about that?"

Precious glanced out of the window. Everett and Boycie stared inside. She smiled at them, wishing she was out there with them.

"It's not a laughing matter," Miss Taylor said. "His mummy has to come in and bring another sandwich. It's a long way for her to walk, and she's poorly."

Say it, say it, say it… Precious shrugged. "Then you lied. He* will *have lunch."*

Miss Taylor's eyebrows moved upwards. She rose from her seat, muttering, "I really don't know what to do with you."

Mummy said that, too. Daddy just laughed and told her to let Precious be.

"You don't have to do anything," Precious said. "Just leave me alone."

"I can't, because what you did was wrong."

Precious prodded a finger into Play-Doh on the table. She wished it was Samuel's eye. "If I say sorry, will it make it all better?" *She'd say it, but she wouldn't mean it.*

"That's a good start. You can speak to Samuel after he comes back inside."

"Can I go out now?"

Miss Taylor sighed. "Go on then."

Precious raced to the cloakroom and changed into her shoes. She put on her coat and ran outside, past Miss Taylor who'd held the door open for her. Everett and Boycie legged it towards her, and they huddled together, their foreheads touching. Mummy said Precious shouldn't do that else she'd get nits.

"What happened?" Everett asked.

"I've got to say sorry to him."

"Easy-peasy." He scanned the playground. "Tomorrow, nick something from his lunch box again."

Precious wasn't scared of Everett, but she had to do what he said or he'd sulk. "All right."

They dashed off to play tag, Everett getting angry at Boycie who caught him easily. Everett didn't like losing, but Daddy said that was a part of life. He'd lost fifty quid at the bookies last night, but he didn't seem bothered. Mummy was, even though he'd said the money wasn't that much of a loss, he had more where that came from.

The bell rang, and they all lined up outside the classroom. Precious hated the way everything had to be done just right. All the rules got on her nerves, and the other day, she'd almost told Miss Taylor to piss off when she'd asked her to put the paintbrushes away.

Precious hadn't been painting, so she didn't see why she had to do it.

They trooped indoors and changed in the cloakroom. Samuel hid in the corner by his peg with its stupid aeroplane picture, his eyes red from crying. Twat. If he wasn't so smelly, he'd still have his sandwich. Miss Taylor appeared in the doorway and sent everyone else into the classroom, leaving Precious and Samuel behind.

"What do you have to say to Samuel?" she asked.

"Sorry for pinching your sandwich," Precious said.

"Good girl. Are you okay, Samuel?"

He shook his head but said, "Yes."

"Mummy's bringing another sandwich, all right?"

His lips wobbled. "But she's got no money, and there were only two bits of bread this morning when she made my lunch."

Miss Taylor looked sad. "Would it be better if I rang Mummy again and told her you can have school dinners today?"

"She won't be able to pay for it."

"That's okay, she doesn't have to. I'll speak to her, because it sounds like you might be able to have free school meals."

That wasn't fair. Why should he have it for nothing when everyone else had to pay? Precious frowned and followed Miss Taylor and Samuel into the classroom. She sat at her table with Everett and Boycie, ready to recite numbers again.

"He's getting free dinners," she said.

Boycie stared over at Samuel. "That means he's poor, my mum told me."

Precious nodded. "He said his mummy didn't have any money."

Miss Taylor clapped. "Right, maths time!"

The day moved on, and at afternoon play, Everett said, "You can't nick his sandwich tomorrow if he's going to have dinners. You should sit by him and steal his pudding instead. Do it when he's not looking. We can share it after."

Boycie laughed. "And tell him he's a big old block of cheese."

Precious smiled, glad she had friends who thought like she did. They weren't scared of getting in trouble either. "But why does it have to be me all the time? Why can't you do it?"

"Because you're the best at it." Everett tapped her arm. "Tag, you're it!"

He ran off, and she chased him, but he was too fast for her. She stopped running and waited for Boycie to catch up.

"I'll do it," he said.

"Do what?"

"Nick Samuel's pudding."

"All right."

They dashed off after Everett again. Boycie knocked into Samuel, sending the kid to the ground. Samuel burst out crying, and one of the mums who worked at the school at playtime came running over.

"I saw that," she said.

"Don't care if you did," Boycie said. "He's a stinky cheese ball."

"That's not very nice. Go and sit on the wall, both of you."

Oh. The wall was where you went if you'd been naughty, and if the headmaster saw you, you got proper told off. Precious went over there with Boycie, and they sat side by side holding hands.

"You're my best friend," he said. "And Everett. Can you come down my end of the street tonight and play? Everett's coming for tea."

"Yeah."

Everett barrelled over, standing in front of them. "What you done?"

"Boycie pushed Samuel over." Precious smiled.

"Good." Everett folded his arms. "I hope he hurt himself."

Precious glanced across at Samuel who walked round with the mum. He held her hand, and with his other, he rubbed his eyes. "Stupid baby." She gave the mum a nasty glare, hating her for sending her to the wall when she hadn't done anything.

When she was a woman, she'd hurt whoever she liked, no one could stop her then. Grown-ups could do anything they wanted, Daddy said.

Mummy and Daddy sat opposite Precious at the dinner table.

"Miss Taylor phoned me after we got home and said you stole from another child today," Mummy said.

Daddy smirked. "Oh dear. Get caught, did you?"

Precious nodded.

Mummy went on to explain benefits and that Samuel's mum got them. "She can't work because she's poorly at the minute, so I want you to be nice to Samuel. Can you be his friend for me?"

"Nah, he's smelly."

"That isn't his fault. Can you be kind?"

"Nah. I don't want to."

Mummy glanced at Daddy who shrugged.

"Look," Daddy said, "just ignore the lad, all right? And try not to get in trouble at school."

"What about at home, though?" Mummy asked him. "The amount of people we have at the front door…"

Daddy tutted. "She's just going through a phase, that's all."

Mummy got up and brought a casserole dish over, placing it on a mat. She lifted the lid, and Precious peered inside. Chicken and vegetables, fat dumplings on the top.

"You're lucky to get breakfast of a morning plus two hot meals a day," Mummy said. "And to have two parents. Samuel's only got one, and he might not get much to eat."

"Not my fault." Precious waited for her dinner to be dished up. "Can I go down the end and play with Boycie after?"

"I'm not sure about that boy." Mummy sat and cut into her dumpling. "You've been naughtier since you made friends with him."

It wasn't Boycie she needed to worry about, Everett was the bossy one. He'd said he was their leader and they were a gang. They were going to grow up and work for him; they'd be best friends forever.

"He's an all right kid," Daddy said.

Mummy sighed. "Okay then, but no getting into mischief."

Precious wasn't going to promise she wouldn't because Boycie had said they were going to nick apples from the old woman who lived next door to him. She had a tree in her back garden, and they'd have to climb up to get them. He reckoned she stank of piss.

"Everett's gone to his house for dinner," Precious said. "Can I have someone to dinner?"

"It depends who it is," Mummy said.

"Boycie or Everett. I don't like anyone else." She'd stopped playing with the ginger girl.

Mummy sighed again. "We'll see."

That meant no. Nothing ever happened when she said 'we'll see'.

"Can I go to theirs for dinner?" Precious asked.

"Maybe."

She ate her dinner quickly, then put her shoes on and ran up the other end of the street. Boycie played out with Everett, kicking a football at the kerb.

A woman came out and glared at them. "Pack it in! That thudding's doing my nut in. Piss off somewhere else and do that."

Boycie poked his tongue out at her. "Fuck off."

"I'll be going to see your mother in a minute if you're not careful. She needs to wash your mouth out

with soap and water." She stomped off inside, slamming her door.

Everett laughed. "Silly cow."

"Come on," Boycie said.

They marched down the side of the old lady's house, Boycie in front, Everett moaning because he was the leader so he ought to go first. He was always doing that, taking charge. Sometimes, Precious wanted to tell him he wasn't the boss, but he'd only get angry if she did.

Boycie opened the squeaky wooden gate and stepped into the garden. Precious and Everett went in, and Boycie shut them inside. He pointed to the big tree and ran over to the back door to peek inside.

"She must be in the front room." He darted to the tree and shimmied up the trunk, throwing red apples down onto the grass.

"We haven't got any bags," Precious said.

Everett held the hem of his T-shirt out. "Put them in there."

Precious bent over to collect the apples, and by the time Boycie got down, the T-shirt bowed, full of fruit. She was about to take her turn to climb up when a screech stopped her.

"Oi, hop it!" a woman shouted.

Precious turned and, spotting the old lady, stuck her fingers up at her. "Piss off!"

"Get out before I call the coppers on you."

Everett waddled to the gate and disappeared down the alley, losing an apple along the way. Boycie went after him, and Precious stared at the old woman.

"Call the police then, see if I care." She walked out slowly, wanting the bitch to say something else so she could shout back at her, but the woman closed her door.

Precious left the gate open on purpose and found Everett and Boycie in the street. Loads of kids had gathered round them, so she had to elbow her way through.

"Ten p each," Everett said. "No money, no apples."

Some kids ran off home to get the dosh, but others wandered away. The ones who were lucky enough to be given ten pence returned. Everett had one pound twenty by the time he'd finished and only one apple left.

He bit into it and said with his mouth full, "I'm going to be rich when I'm older."

Boycie glared at him. "I did the nicking, so that money's mine."

"I did the selling, so up yours." Everett slid the coins in his pocket. "I'm going home." He ran off.

Precious stared after him. "Pig," she shouted.

Everett laughed. "You won't be calling me that when I make you rich, too."

She turned to Boycie. "Shall we nick some more?"

He nodded. "But we'll have to go to the next street to sell them."

Precious thought about that. Mummy said she mustn't leave their road. But since when had she cared about following rules? "All right then."

They grinned and skipped off towards the garden.

Chapter Seven

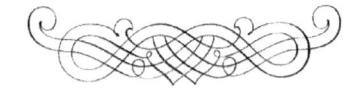

Goddess had bitten off more than she could chew, she'd known that a while ago. The problem was, Farah wouldn't take no for an answer. She ran the escort agency with Joseph. The real reason Goddess had left that job was because she didn't feel comfortable working for the couple anymore. The normal side of the escort business didn't allow any sexual conduct whatsoever, but behind that façade was a depraved side she hadn't wanted to participate in. That side was at a warehouse.

She'd refused a job there, a place that came alive at night, full of men wanting to have sex with dancers in cages that lined the two side walls. At the back stood a bar where punters could drink to their heart's content while watching other customers having sex in full view of everybody else. In the centre stood a stage, questionable sexual acts occurring, a free-for-all that had churned her stomach. Each to their own, but it wasn't her scene.

Farah had taken Goddess there to show her what she could be doing and how much she'd be earning if she agreed. Goddess didn't want that kind of attention. Yes, she had sex with men and they paid her for it, but she was still in control. In the warehouse, she'd have none of that. People would paw her, she'd have no choice but to accept it so long as they put tenners in the strap of her knickers or in the cups of her bra for the privilege.

As she wasn't struck on that kind of work, she'd politely declined and had handed in her notice, going to work at the Lantern instead. Farah hadn't liked the rejection. And while Goddess had promised not to mention to anyone what happened in the warehouse, it seemed Farah didn't trust her enough that she'd keep her mouth shut. In order to be 'set free', as it were, Goddess had to find new recruits for the warehouse, customers and sex workers alike. George and Greg wouldn't think twice about slicing her face if they found out she'd crossed them. But the thing was, Joseph was just as scary, so she was stuck between two evils.

At the Lantern, she'd asked for everyone's phone numbers, making out they could all be friends, and then passed them on to Farah so she could contact the women directly about the warehouse work, although thankfully, she hadn't told them where she'd got the numbers from. Goddess thought it was obvious, though, or maybe she just felt guilty.

She asked herself often why she'd walked into this line of work. Why she hadn't married the man who'd asked her dad for permission when she'd been eighteen. Why she'd walked away from the solid dependability of suburbia into the unpredictable, sometimes scary world of sex.

Her decisions in life had always been questionable. She knew what was right for her and what she should do, but her brain always told her to do the opposite. Now she'd convinced herself that the only love she would receive was via touches from men who paid her to do the deed—no one would want her now, she was too tainted. She'd never have a steady, proper relationship where no money changed hands. She accepted she'd never be 'normal'.

Still nervous, having been picked up by Farah and Joseph earlier, Goddess sat at the bar in the warehouse. She could say they'd brought her here against her will, but of course she'd agreed to go, fearing what Joseph might do if she didn't. It was easier that way, to obey what he said. They knew where she lived, they knew where she worked, so there was no hiding from them. What Goddess didn't know was how long it was going to take for Farah to trust her, therefore letting her go.

Don't be stupid. That's just an excuse she's using.

As long as they had her at the Orange Lantern to steer customers towards the warehouse, they were never going to let her go. She'd toyed with the idea of telling Widow, who could then tell the twins, but Joseph, who was a particularly nasty piece of work, had already warned her not to go down that road. He didn't do Cheshire grins like George, he completely ruined faces instead. He crisscrossed them so the skin looked like a roasted gammon, so he'd described, diamonds all over it. That would mean the end of her career. The end of her life, really, because she couldn't walk around as ugly as that. Call her vain, but she couldn't bear to be disfigured.

The warehouse was currently empty of customers. Only the woman who oversaw the sex workers was there, plus the barman who stocked up ready for tonight's 'party'. Each customer had to say a special password before they'd be let in. Each party had a different password. Farah stupidly thought that would keep the police out, and Goddess wondered whether the woman had any brains at all. A customer in possession of the password could easily pass it on to the police. She doubted the coppers around here would turn a blind eye to such deliberate disregard of the law.

All she wanted was to cut ties with Farah and Joseph. She wished she'd never worked at the escort agency, but she hadn't had a bloody choice; another person also pulled her strings. The married couple were just using her now, an employee they didn't need to pay who drummed up business, all because they'd threatened to do something awful if she didn't. They'd ensured Goddess would do as she was told.

She had no idea why they'd brought her here today. They hadn't said, just that she had to phone in sick at the Lantern. She could only imagine they were going to persuade — or force her — to work at the party. She wouldn't mind if it was as a topless waitress, but she wasn't prepared to join what amounted to a massive orgy. She preferred to entertain punters in her own room, in privacy, and had never been an exhibitionist.

As Joseph had gone out the back to check the alcohol stock, Goddess leaned towards Farah and asked quietly, "Is there any particular reason I'm here? Because I told you I didn't want to get involved with this side of your business and I thought you understood that. I've done what you wanted, and I gave you all the girls' phone numbers from the Lantern. Plus I tell every customer there that they should come here." She had a feeling that certain passwords had been given only to her so they could tell whether she'd actually enticed customers in or not.

"Your loyalty isn't in question," Farah said. "But we believe you'd be a big draw. From what we've heard, you've doubled the amount of punters that go to the Lantern. People sense that you're a sexual being and they can't wait to be in your company."

Goddess was well aware that this was just a crappy spiel to make out they thought she was special. They didn't really think of her as a 'sexual being' who attracted others, it was all about money and how much she could generate for them. If she wanted to do this line of work, of course she'd be happy to jump in and have sex in the warehouse, but she didn't so…

"I don't want to do it. I like it at the Lantern. If I don't want to entertain a particular customer there, then I don't have to. I'd have no choice here. I'd be touched when I didn't want to be. No one would understand the word no." *A bit like you because you keep on and on at me to come to these fucking creepy parties.*

"If we promised you that you wouldn't be touched and you could just walk around and greet people, would you reconsider?"

Goddess thought of Precious and how she flirted with the customers when they arrived at the Lantern. She took them into the living room and got them geed up for the women workers upstairs. It wasn't a bad line of work because she never got touched either. But Goddess didn't trust the type of men who'd come here. Then again, Joseph likely had security everywhere, and if anyone put a foot wrong, they'd be thrown out. Prior to that, they'd probably be beaten up.

She couldn't do it, but she'd have to play this carefully so she didn't get Farah's back up. "I don't know. I don't like the idea of the warehouse and everything it represents. Who has the control? Where's the safety of the women? How packed does it get? Are there cameras security can watch to spot when bad things are happening? Are the workers safe?" She clocked Farah's expression so rushed to say, "Of course you've got all that covered, I just wanted answers."

"It'll be one hundred people at the most. Look at the size of this place. We can see everything going on with that amount of people. You'll be safe; all you'll be doing is walking round, flirting.

People will come here just so you spoke to them. I don't think you realise how beautiful you are."

She makes me sound like some siren when I'm not. "I'd rather just stay where I am, thank you. I can pick and choose my hours there. And if I don't want to work nights, then I don't have to. I'm protected by The Brothers."

"You'd be protected by us."

It's hardly the fucking same, is it? "I know, but I'll stick with the job I have."

Farah's nostrils flared with her intake of breath. "Fair enough. I'll drive you home."

Goddess didn't trust that Farah would end it there. The couple had been so insistent that she worked for them, that for her to just drop it now without a fight didn't make sense. Goddess worried that they'd hurt her. They'd come for her tonight or send someone round. But if she went to the Lantern and did her shift, she'd be safe until two in the morning when it ended.

Maybe she ought to get hold of the twins and tell them everything. *Not everything. Just some things...* They could deal with it, and then she wouldn't have to worry about that particular problem, just all the others.

She followed Farah out of the warehouse and sat in the back seat of the SUV. Farah took her home as promised, although she didn't speak for the whole journey. Goddess suspected she was supposed to feel like she'd done something wrong, or that she should fill the silence or promise she'd work at the warehouse, but she was stronger than that, at least in this scenario.

She walked up her garden path as the SUV drove away, pausing when her neighbour, Oaklynn, came out of her house with her baby on her hip.

"The twins have been here," Oaklynn said, walloped on the side of the head by her son's soft rattle. "Oi, that's enough, young man." She sighed. "I'm not going to lie, I told them the number plate of the car you went in. This has gone far enough, and seeing as you aren't going to do something about it, I did. Those two shouldn't be able to treat you like they do just because you worked for them once."

Several times, Oaklynn had told Goddess to tell The Brothers about the married couple. She'd said it was best to come clean rather than them find out later down the line and blame her for keeping secrets.

"It's about time you told them, don't you think?" Oaklynn stroked the baby's hair. "They're worried about you. Greg said they'd come to see if you were okay, whether you'd called in sick. I said I didn't think you were poorly. I'm sorry if you think I've stepped over the line, but this has got to come to an end. I didn't tell them who Farah and Joseph are, they'll probably find that out via the number plate. But you need to give them a ring and let them know you're okay. Or not, as the case may be."

Paranoid for a moment, Goddess inspected Oaklynn's words. Had she been referring to someone else entirely with the "or not"? Did she know Goddess had more to worry about than Farah and Joseph?

Oh God, was she told to get friendly with me so she can keep tabs?

Goddess recalled when Oaklynn had knocked on the door and asked her if she fancied a cuppa. It had been just after…just after the thing Goddess tried hard not to think about. It worked with the timeline.

Thank God I've never told her what's really going on. I'd be in so much trouble then if she passed along what I'd said.

Oaklynn jerked her head towards the kerb as if the SUV was still there. "What did those two fuckers want this time?"

"They took me to the warehouse again. She tried to persuade me to work there. She reckons I won't even get touched, that I just need to flirt with people, but for God's sake, someone's going to touch me, and it's gross when it isn't on my terms. She just said 'fair enough' and brought me home, but I don't think she's accepted my decision at all. And I'd already decided to let the twins know what was going on. I don't want to lose my job at the Lantern."

She'd purposely come across as being up her own arse and snobby. She thought if she had an air about her, she'd be left alone. No one would want to get too close and ask questions—ones she wasn't allowed to answer.

"I'm just glad you've made the right decision," Oaklynn said. "Honestly, those two need to be stopped. I mean, the escort agency is okay, but that warehouse…"

"I'll go and phone the twins now. Thanks for being there for me."

So she didn't cry in front of her, Goddess quickly walked up her path and opened the front door. She reminded herself, yet again, to get the glass changed. She'd never liked the fact that people could see straight in. That was the reason Farah had known she was home this morning, because she'd looked through and spotted Goddess at the kitchen sink.

She closed the door and drew the curtain across. From now on, until she got new glass, she'd always close it. She walked into the living room and did the same there, then pulled the blinds in the kitchen. If it meant hiding for a while, that was fine. And anyway, if the twins sorted Farah and Joseph, then she'd never have to worry about them again, and one of her missions would have been ticked off the list.

She found their number in her phone and instead of ringing, she sent a message.

GODDESS: I NEED TO SPEAK TO YOU URGENTLY. I'M AT HOME NOW. IS THERE ANY CHANCE YOU CAN COME IN DISGUISE OR AROUND THE BACK WAY? I HAVE A FEELING I'M BEING WATCHED. OR MAYBE I CAN COME AND MEET YOU SOMEWHERE.

GG: WHO IS THIS?

GODDESS: SORRY, IT'S GODDESS. MY NEIGHBOUR SAID YOU WERE ROUND MINE EARLIER.

GG: Right. We'll arrive in a black cab so it'll look like you ordered one. We'll take you for a ride and you can tell us what the problem is. For the record, we already knew you were at home. If you look out the front, there's a man sitting in a red car.

She moved the curtain a bit and glanced outside. She hadn't spotted him when Farah had dropped her off, nor when she'd been speaking to Oaklynn, so maybe he'd lowered himself in his seat.

Goddess: I see him. Why's he here?

GG: Because we wanted to check whether you were on the level or not. Word on the street is you're hanging around with some dodgy people. I hope you plan to explain that to us.

Goddess: I do.

GG: Our taxi is five minutes away. We'll have beards, wigs, and glasses on. Greg will be in the back seat so it'll look like a rideshare should anyone else be watching. Our man hasn't spotted anybody, though.

She thought about how she'd put her case across so she came off in the best light. But she hadn't really done anything wrong. All she'd done was pass information along to punters about a sex party. But would the twins see it that way? Would they see it that she was trying to prevent people from coming into the Lantern and sending them to the warehouse instead? Would they say she was sabotaging their business?

She'd have to wait and see, but fucking hell, she was shitting her knickers.

They arrived shortly after she'd changed into a light-grey tracksuit and trainers, stuffing her hair into a top bun. She left her house carrying her small pink sports holdall, so if Farah had sent someone to watch her, they'd think she was going to the gym. That wasn't an unusual occurrence; it wouldn't look suspicious. As she opened the back door of the taxi, she glanced to her left at the man in the red car. He nodded to her, and she nodded back. She climbed in and put her seat belt on, placing her bag between herself and Greg.

She'd seen the twins a few times at the Lantern, and they'd scared her a bit then, but now she was terrified. She was stuck in close proximity to two monsters. All Greg would need to do was flick out his fist and he could break her nose. Funny how these two were still her best bet. Farah and Joseph aside, the *other* person directing her life had to also be considered as a threat.

But what if the other person is watching and they think I'm going to the twins behind their back? Should I message and let them know why I'm doing this? Or would it be obvious, considering the instructions I've been given?

George drove away. His window was open a little, and the breeze stirred his long ginger beard. It reminded her of Farah's hair, and she shivered.

"Did someone walk over your grave?" He watched her in the rearview mirror. "Because if they didn't, then you've clearly just shat yourself. Now I know our reputation precedes us, but why would you be scared of us when you've met us before? So unless you've done something wrong…"

"Stop frightening her, you twat," Greg said. "How do you expect her to tell you anything if you worry the shit out of her? Behave yourself for five minutes, will you?"

Thankful Greg had stepped in, Goddess turned and smiled at him. "I don't really know how to start so I may as well just say it how it is and you can decide what to do with me after."

"That doesn't sound good," Greg said.

"I'm hoping you won't see what I've done as anything bad. But I'm not you, I don't know what goes on in your head, so…" She took a deep breath and got herself together. "The escort agency I worked for is run by the people who picked me up today. They're called Joseph and Farah Bains, but I expect you know that by now."

"Yep, go on," George said.

"It's a legitimate business, and it's true that I didn't have to have sex with anyone. That's not what's on offer, not there anyway. Before I started at the Lantern, Farah asked me if I wanted to work in their warehouse. I wasn't sure what she meant so she took me there to show me. All I can say is that it's basically a sex party where anyone can have sex with anyone. I suppose there's a fee that's paid at the front door; I don't know anything about that, I never asked. But she wanted me to work there because she said I'd pull in a lot of customers. I didn't want to do it."

"To be fair, she's got a point about the pulling in of customers," George said.

"For fuck's sake, bruv," Greg muttered.

"Sorry. I'll shut up."

Goddess smiled, despite being uneasy. "So she said I had to find customers. Those two are so weird that I didn't feel I could say no. Joseph's an arsehole and hurts people if they don't do what he wants. He cuts women's faces."

"Cunt," George whispered.

"Pot calling the kettle black?" Greg asked him.

"You know what I meant," George said. "It sounds like he does it for fun, not as a lesson." He glanced at her in the mirror again. "So they run this orgy at a warehouse, do they?" He drummed his fingertips on the centre of the steering wheel. "And where is this warehouse?"

She gave them the address, and he seemed pleased. Why? Did they already know where it was and he'd asked to see if she lied to them? So she didn't dwell on that, she told them what had happened today and how Farah had seemed to accept the fact that Goddess didn't want to be involved.

"But she wouldn't just let me go like that. I don't trust her. I think someone will be watching me now and they'll maybe try to hurt me because I've gone against what they want."

"They won't be able to get hold of you because you'll be in hiding," George said. "That fella in the red car outside your house will go with you. We have several safe houses, so you'll go to one of those. You can go home once it's all over."

Relief smacked into her. "How long will that be?"

"We try to be as quick as possible, but take a couple of books just in case." He chuckled. "There's a telly and whatever. Think of it as a holiday."

"Am I in trouble for not telling you sooner?"

"I'm not going to pretend it hasn't pissed me off because it has. But if you thought your life was in danger, then we can understand you keeping your mouth shut. And you've told us now, so that's the main thing. I'm not liking the sound of this couple. They seem money greedy and unhinged. Having seen the size of their house, I have to say that the sex industry's paying them extremely well."

Shocked they'd done so much, so soon, she said, "You've been to their *house*?"

"We like to know who we're dealing with so we get a feel for them before we make our approach. Me and Greg still need to have a little chat about how we're going to deal with them. They've broken the rules, so they'll have to be punished for that. They owe us a lot of protection money."

"What do you normally do to people who forget to pay it?"

"Oh, they haven't forgotten. It's deliberate, but we usually give them a beating, set up a payment arrangement, and then if they forget again, the punishment is worse. I'll leave you to work out what that is."

She'd heard they killed people, but for him to basically say it...

"We'll drop you off at the Lantern for now. If you can explain everything to Widow, because she's got a cob on with you not texting her about your shifts."

"I panicked when Farah and Joseph turned up. Jessica was the first one I could think of to contact. I know it should have been Widow, but that's not how it turned out, and I can't change that. Will I still have a job?" She couldn't afford to lose it, not yet. She had things to do there before she could walk away.

"We'll make sure you do, but you won't be working today, we just need you to look like you're going to. The red light will remain on outside your door, so if any punters are sent in to see what's going on, it'll seem like you're entertaining. We'll make arrangements for the man in the red car to pick you up round the back. His name's Will."

"Thank you," she said, relieved this had been taken out of her hands. How would she get hold of some everyday clothes for when she stayed at the safe house? She didn't exactly want to take anything from her wardrobe at the Lantern, it was hardly appropriate. "What about my stuff? I'll need clean knickers and whatever. A toothbrush."

"Tell me your sizes, and Will can go and pick some gear up from Tesco."

She let out a slow sigh, wishing she'd done this ages ago. If she'd known it would be this easy, she'd never have done what the Bains couple wanted. Could she ask for the twins' help a second time once this part was over? Could she fully put her trust in them so they could end the nightmare she'd found herself living because of that other person?

Chapter Eight

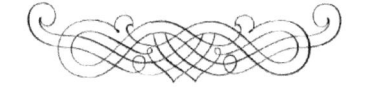

Kayla Barnes had been feeling uneasy ever since Roach's death. Even though she'd kept under the radar, living with her boyfriend, Cooper, and going to work like any other innocent person, something didn't feel right. Sometimes she thought she was being watched while in her flat, but that was stupid. It was too high up for anyone to nose through her windows unless they stood on the balcony out the front, so it would have to be someone from the opposite homes staring across the street at her. But why would they do that?

Luckily, her life hadn't completely gone to shit, not that it really was shit, she just liked to dramatise things. Cooper was now running his own little drug empire, selling to all of Roach's previous customers. He'd got in contact with a big dealer The Brothers had recommended who was prepared to sell to him in large quantities, based on him knowing Boycie, and so far his business venture had thrived. It meant he had lots of money, and now their flat, which Roach had owned, was filled with all the furniture she'd had her eye on for months. She'd blinged it right up.

Boycie had popped by to tell her that the flats and Roach's house had been left to him, he just had to wait for them to be signed over to him officially. He was now their new landlord. She didn't mind, he was a nice enough bloke if you didn't get on his bad side. She was pissed off, though, when he'd told her the brothel was no longer on the table as somewhere she could work.

The twins had taken over. Her dream of earning a good wage there had been taken away from her—because there was no way George and Greg would want her anywhere near the place.

She'd been going to the park a lot for lunch, over the road from her office. She hated the sound of the kids there, they screeched too much, but it saved her from having to eat in the staffroom or go to the pub with colleagues she didn't much like. They weren't fond of Cooper, so therefore, they could go and fuck themselves. It was at the park that she felt watched the most, and rather than stay away, she kept going back to see if she could catch out whoever it was.

At first, she'd sworn it was the drug dealer who stood by the gate and handed over wraps in secret handshakes. Then she swore it was the homeless man who lay out on the bench all day. But the more she thought about it, the more she reckoned it was the woman with the blue hair and super-dark sunglasses who came and sat on a nearby bench but never had any kids with her. Maybe she wasn't anyone to worry about. She could also work in an office and spend her lunch break in the park, although she never ate anything. *Was* she the one Kayla had to worry about?

Or am I paranoid?

She hadn't factored in that helping to kill Alice would affect her so much.

Kayla sat in the park now, hidden by a few trees. The woman wasn't there yet, but she didn't usually arrive until half an hour after Kayla. It was weird because she seemed familiar, yet Kayla had never seen her before until she'd started coming to the park. Maybe she had mannerisms that reminded her of someone else, but she couldn't think who that might be. She hated it when her brain hid things from her.

Halfway through her tuna and sweetcorn sandwich, she caught movement from the corner of her eye. Blue Hair had arrived and had the gall to sit right next to her this time. Kayla wasn't putting up with this bollocks and, seeing as she was never one to back down from anything, unless it was the twins threatening her, she'd have to put this bitch straight. She wanted to get to the bottom of it.

"Look, have you been watching me lately?" Kayla asked. The woman had as much entitlement to come to the park as she did, but it just felt so *odd*.

"Excuse me?" Blue Hair barked. "Why would I want to come and watch *you*? Talk about think you're special. Entitled much?"

Fuck off. "It's just that you stare over at me."

"I didn't even realise I was doing it. Fucking hell, can't anyone just stare into space anymore without the politically correct brigade clutching their pearls about it?"

"All right, why come and sit right next to me today when you don't usually do that?"

"Bloody hell, I'll move, okay?"

She wandered over towards the homeless man's bench. He pulled his knees towards his stomach to make more room for her, and she sat at the end. Kayla remembered the time she'd pushed him off onto the ground and how cruel she'd been to him. She still didn't feel guilty about it even now. He was a stinky, scummy bastard hooked on drink and drugs, most likely. He'd told her he lived in the night shelter, and she'd told him to have a bath or something like that. She was quite proud of how nasty she could be. Weird, because she hadn't been brought up that way. Mum had never got over Kayla's spite.

Blue Hair offered him half of her sandwich.

Kayla chuffed out a laugh. "Bloody Nora, she's a right do-gooder."

She got up and walked towards the exit, popping her sandwich packet in the bin closest to the bench. She gave Blue Hair a filthy look, just to get her to say something so they could interact again, so she'd admit she'd been watching Kayla, but the woman ignored her, too busy biting into a red apple.

Angry her ploy hadn't worked, Kayla continued through the exit, down the pavement towards the office. She glanced across the street at a man with sunglasses and a baseball cap pulled low. She couldn't see his eyes so couldn't tell if he was looking directly at her, but it felt like it. Was she going mad? Was she imagining people staring when they weren't? *Was* it the guilt of the part she'd played in Alice's death? She'd watched *The Muppets Christmas Carol* and understood its meaning. Was the ghost of the past coming for *her* now? Did she have to become a nice and generous person in order to be forgiven?

She laughed at the thought of that and carried on towards work. At her desk, she sighed at the amount of new jobs that had come in while she'd been out. She hated it here, but she wasn't confident enough in Cooper's career to give up work yet. Besides, she enjoyed her bit of independence and having her own money. She didn't want anyone to have control over what she spent, so despite whinging and moaning about having to come to work, she'd carry on regardless. Anyway, the future was never certain, and she wasn't sure that Cooper would stick around. He'd shown no sign of wanting to leave her so far, and he was always encouraging and kind to her, but you never could tell when the worm was going to turn. Best she safeguard herself by keeping her own income.

Four hours later, she left work to walk towards the bus stop. That man was there again, the one in the sunglasses and baseball cap. He spoke to the blue-haired woman, and it freaked Kayla out so much she ran the other way. She headed for the taxi rank around the corner, jumping into the first one in the queue and telling the driver where to take her. All the way home, she panicked that the couple were watching her from inside another vehicle that followed the cab. Who were they? Why would they even *be* watching her? But it was too much of a coincidence for them to have both been there again.

Once she got home, she ran indoors, relieved to find Cooper lying on the sofa watching TV.

"What the fuck's up with you?" he asked.

"You know I said that woman with the blue hair's watching me? Well, I saw her again today at the park. She sat right next to me this time, so I outright asked her what she was playing at. Anyway, she fobbed me off. And then when I left the park I saw this bloke; *he* was watching me, too. I left work, and they were both in the street together. Now come on, something weird is going on. Have you done something that might make someone want to scare me to get back at you? Do you owe your dealer for drugs?"

"Talk about paranoid," he said. "No one would dare fuck me or you about. I use Roach's name and legacy to get by, I've got Boycie on hand, and the twins know I'm dealing and take protection money off me. No one will cross me, you know that. They think I'm as scary as them."

"Then why are they watching me? I'm not paranoid, I swear."

"I don't know, but maybe you should take some time off work. Come out with me during the evening instead."

"I can't have more time off, I already took loads when I went to stay at Haven. My boss isn't going keep putting up with me saying I'm depressed."

"But if you've got a doctor's note, there's nothing he can do about it."

"No, it'll be fine. I'll ask if I can work from home instead."

"Will you come out with me in the evening anyway? I'm always here in the day so I can look after you while you work from home, but at night…I don't want to leave you on your own."

Kayla had never had anyone care for her like Cooper did. Okay, her parents had, but she'd taken that for granted and treated them like shit. He might look rough and ready, he might be common, but he was so nice to her. But would she have enough energy to go to work all day, cook dinner, and then go out selling drugs at night? She wasn't worried about the twins seeing her with Cooper because he'd done the right thing by telling them he was now a seller, but for some reason, she hated the thought of them looking down their noses at her, as if she'd allowed herself to be 'less than' by being with Cooper. Or were they her mother's words getting inside her head?

Mum wouldn't have chosen Cooper as Kayla's boyfriend. She'd likely imagined someone in a suit and tie and posh shiny shoes with a job that meant he got a company car. Kayla wasn't who Mum had expected her to be either. Perhaps if the expectations hadn't been so high, Kayla might well have turned out to be a normal person. But the pressure from her parents had meant she'd rebelled and done everything they wouldn't have wanted her to just to prove the point this was *her* life and she could do what she wanted.

Even down to helping Precious murder Alice.

Kayla had lured Alice to the hairdresser's. In a court of law, she'd be just as liable as if she'd pulled the trigger. It would be one of those joint enterprise things. But she had no intention of anyone finding out what she'd done. No one knew where Vicky Hart was, the woman she'd pretended to be who'd made friends with Alice at Haven. She'd disappeared, and the twins had discovered that her name had been borrowed from some bird in Essex. The real Vicky didn't have a clue about anything going on in the East End. Only a few people knew Kayla had been Vicky, and as long as they kept their mouths shut, everything would be okay.

It still didn't solve the fact she was being watched, though.

Oh God, had the twins put two and two together and realised she was Vicky? Was she under surveillance for the ideal time to snatch her away to wherever they tortured people?

She rushed into the kitchen to hide the fear that must be on her face. She didn't want Cooper worrying. But what if she was living on borrowed time? What if the clock was now ticking towards the moment of her death?

"Stop being so dramatic," she whispered.

But she honestly felt that this time the drama was real, not something she'd deliberately fabricated.

Chapter Nine

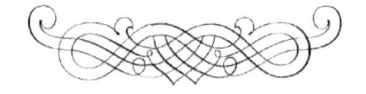

Precious couldn't believe how things had worked out in her favour, when at first, it had seemed like it wouldn't—because Boycie had decided to stay at his place tonight, even though she'd asked him to kip at hers for an alibi. She supposed he was making a point that *she* couldn't tell *him* what to do either. If he wanted to be pathetic and play games, he could get on with it; she could deal with Edna and Kayla by herself. The only worry she had was whether Boycie was still going to say they'd been together should she ever be asked where she'd been after work.

She stood on the balcony outside her flat, leaning over the railing to watch Boycie getting into his car. Kayla and Cooper came out of their gaff along the way.

"Are you sure you don't want to put your big puffa jacket on?" Cooper asked. "It gets colder later on."

"God, you sound like my mum," Kayla snapped. "I've got a gilet on under my coat so I'll be fine. Are you going to be fussing like this all night, because if you are, I think I'd rather stay home."

"You're not staying home with that creepy blue-haired bitch hanging around."

That would be me in a wig.

Precious hid her smirk as the couple came towards her. Then she waved at Boycie when he drove off. Thank God he hadn't hung around for a couple of minutes longer. He'd have known then that Kayla had rumbled her. Maybe she'd also rumbled Boycie earlier today. He'd at least agreed to watch Kayla with her, but the silly cow had run the other way instead of getting the bus. They'd planned to get on the same one and follow her all the way home just to put the shits up her, but things hadn't panned out that way.

"Everything all right, Kayla?" Precious asked in her normal voice, nothing like the one she used as Blue Hair. "You look a bit pale."

"God, something weird has been going on." Kayla glanced at Cooper as if to ask for permission to tell Precious about it. At his nod, she looked at Precious. "Ever since Roach died, I've had this really weird feeling that I'm being watched, followed even. Anyway, today I spoke to this woman with blue hair. She comes to the park when I go there for lunch, and she stares at me a lot. Well, she said she doesn't and she got really pissed off with me and stomped off. But then I saw this bloke, and he stared, too."

For all of his talk that Precious had fucked up by letting Kayla see her watching and staring, Boycie hadn't done so well in that department either, then. Precious would have great pleasure in letting him know that.

Kayla carried on. "After work, I saw them both together. I mean, what are the odds of that? I don't think it's a coincidence, do you?"

"It does sound odd," Precious said, "but would someone with distinctive blue hair be following you? Wouldn't you have thought whoever it was would be more inconspicuous?"

"That's true," Cooper said. "We hadn't thought of that."

"Blue hair or not, she's still staring," Kayla said. "Anyway, if she thinks she can do anything to me, she's made a mistake because I'll be working with Cooper every night now."

"Why do you think she'd do anything to you?" Precious asked. "Are you maybe being a bit paranoid?"

"He keeps calling me that." Kayla jabbed a thumb at Cooper. "But I'm not. I swear to God I'm being watched and followed. I actually think someone knows what I did and they're after me. It could even be the twins."

Precious shrugged. "I doubt it. They'd have picked you up way before now. Well, you know where I am if you need me, but remember, I work until the early hours so might not be able to talk if you ring. What area will you be in this evening?

I can ask Boycie to drive by to make sure you're both okay. All right, he was going home to watch the telly, but he won't mind if I ask him."

"Nah," Cooper said. "We don't want to put anybody out. And besides, I can handle it. See ya."

The couple walked off down the stairs, and Precious seethed at not knowing which drug patch they were going to be at. She had enough time to follow them now and find out, but Boycie would say it wasn't advisable to kill tonight, not when Kayla had Cooper with her. He'd likely be more observant and spot her spying. She leaned over the railing again. They came out from the bottom of the stairs and walked over the communal grass towards his car. They got in, and he drove off, Precious watching until the taillights disappeared around the corner.

She returned inside her flat, her mind going a mile a minute, scrabbling to get a plan in order. No matter what Boycie would say, this was too good an opportunity to miss. She could go to Edna any night, but Kayla had always presented a problem in when and how Precious would kill her. If she was working with Cooper in the evenings, it would make it easier to grab hold of her. The issue was, would Kayla still be out at three in the morning when Precious left work? Then she had to factor in the time it took to get to wherever Kayla was.

Maybe she should listen to Boycie's voice in her head and not be so hasty.

But there's time before I start work.

Kill her, kill her, kill her…

There were only two drug patches Cooper worked frequently. She reckoned he'd be at the bigger one that drew in the most money. He'd be busy ordering his runners around, and Kayla would likely be sitting on the nearby bench. If Precious played her cards right, she could creep up behind Kayla while Cooper was occupied, slice her throat, and melt back into the shadows. Obviously there was no CCTV on the streets Cooper worked, he wouldn't be stupid enough to get caught that way, so all she had to do was be careful no one witnessed the murder. That would be difficult, seeing as a row of houses stood opposite the bench. And what if Cooper stood by it or even sat with her instead of standing on the pavement like he usually did? Would he want to leave Kayla sitting alone with trees behind her? Wouldn't he want to make sure she was safe?

While it was crazy for Precious to move forward with this tonight, it gave her a big thrill to contemplate doing something like this again. She used to be on hand to help Roach in these situations, and she was good enough at what she did in the darkness to get away with it. She already had the escape route mapped out from when she'd murdered someone there before. That had been put down to a drug deal gone wrong, so maybe the police would think the same this time.

She'd take the warren of alleyways through the housing estate and come out near the road that led to the Orange Lantern. If she was careful, she wouldn't get blood on her, and she'd wear her three-quarter-length coat with the interchangeable sides. Black for the murder, red for walking into the Lantern. Underneath it, she'd have on her red basque and thick black tights, and it'd look as if she'd dressed that way for work.

She went into her bedroom to get ready, her mind made up. There'd be no changing it now. She went through the murder in her head. She'd base it on the one she done there previously, and so long as Cooper or his runners didn't put a spanner in the works, she'd get away with it.

Dressed, she slid her feet into her trainers. It wasn't unusual for her to wear them to and from work as she changed into her high-heeled shoes once she got there. The only thing that wouldn't look right would be her hair as she'd have had a balaclava on. She put it in a bun and slipped a small folding comb in her left pocket, the flick-knife in the right. She could tidy her barnet up later. With a bumbag strapped to her stomach beneath her jacket, she placed her phone inside it, switched off, plus her keys and the balaclava, and left the flat with the red side of her jacket on show, gloves on.

She couldn't take her car, a taxi, or the bus to see which patch they were on, so she had to walk. She couldn't risk any number plates being caught on camera. As she approached the first patch, she stepped into a bricked enclosure containing wheelie bins and switched her coat to the black side. Balaclava on, she emerged and sidled along to peer around the corner. Two of Cooper's sellers stood beneath a lamppost, dealing to a kid who may also be a runner, but if he wasn't, he was far too young to be an addict.

She'd picked the wrong place and should have gone with her instincts.

She turned and walked away, heading for the second patch, the one with the bench. Of course he'd have gone there; it was the busiest and needed the most observation. Aware she'd be noticed in her balaclava but not willing to show her face, she kept to the shadows again. She crept along the farthest edge of the tree line, watching the scene between the trunks ahead of her. She spied Kayla sitting on the bench, looking down at her phone. Cooper stood on the pavement about a hundred metres away with three of his runners, their heads bent in conversation. This was the ideal time to get the job done. Would she succeed in time before Kayla screamed? It was a risk she was prepared to take. If she had to, she'd slice Cooper and the runners, too.

She took her flick-knife out of her pocket and released the blade, holding it down by her side. As silently as she could, she walked over the short grass, keeping her eye on Cooper and his runners. They seemed in too deep a discussion to be bothered about her.

Lucky me.

She smiled and dashed forward. Kayla had earbuds in. Maybe Cooper had told her to wear them so she didn't hear what they were saying. Or maybe she was that dumb, she didn't think anyone would have the guts to come up behind her like this. Knife lifted, Precious gripped Kayla's hair and tipped her head back. The blade cut through the skin of her neck easily, and as Precious drew it away from the throat, she held her arm out and flicked blood off. She didn't have time to admire her handiwork. She snatched up Kayla's phone and switched it off, sliding it into her pocket. She retreated into the tree line, moving some distance away so she could still watch from behind a tree but could leg it, unseen, if Cooper or his runners came her way. She studied Kayla who'd flopped sideways, her temple resting on the seat of the bench. Cooper was still talking. She couldn't believe how he was supposed to be looking after his girlfriend and had failed so miserably.

What an absolute bellend.

Sick of the sight of him, Precious weaved through the trees until she got to a place of relative safety, a thick cluster of bushes in front of her. She stepped to the side and bent low to wiggle the blade in a stream that ran behind the tree line. Satisfied it was clean, she folded it up and placed it in her pocket. She walked out into a residential street and hurried along with her head bent and her hands in her pockets. If anyone looked out of their windows they would see someone in a balaclava and might phone the police, so she had to get a move on. She dipped down an alley into someone's back garden. Hiding down the side of their shed, she turned her jacket around to the red side, took her balaclava off, and popped it in her pocket along with the gloves. She combed her hair, put it back in a bun, then left the garden, trotting along as if she didn't have a care in the world.

Funny that, because she didn't.

She glanced at her watch to check if she'd be at work on time. It turned out she'd actually be early. That wasn't unusual for her either. And besides, it would only be ten minutes. She continued on, imagining Cooper discovering Kayla. Would he phone The Brothers for help, or would he choose the police? It would be interesting to find out which option he'd go with. He might even knock on Precious' door at some point and tell her Kayla was dead. She'd enjoy that.

She reached the Orange Lantern with her head as clear as her conscience. There was no choice here, Kayla and Edna needed to die in order for her to be safe. She tapped on the door, expecting one of the women to answer, but a man did. What was a customer doing, letting her in? Maybe he was just on his way out. She spied Charmaine at the end of the hallway leaving the kitchen with a cup of tea. She must be on her break. Precious glanced at the man, who still hadn't fucked off. She stepped inside and walked towards Charmaine.

"What the fuck's *he* doing?" Precious asked.

"His name's Cameron, and The Brothers sent him. Something's going on, and they'd rather be safe than sorry."

"*What's* going on?"

"No idea. Widow hasn't said. What she *did* say was we needed to mind our own business and get on with our jobs."

Precious went to the large wardrobe in the kitchen to take her trainers off and switch them for her work shoes. She used the mirror on the inside of the wardrobe door to fix her hair, then popped her head into the office to look at tonight's schedule. She didn't ask Widow what was going on, just saying hello, feeling it best to stay beneath the radar, especially after what she'd been up to before she'd got here. But Widow had other ideas.

"That man out there is here for security," she said. "One of the women might be in danger, so the twins have made sure she's safe."

Precious didn't give a fiddler's fuck which woman it was but reckoned she'd better ask anyway. It might look weird if she didn't. "Who is it?"

"Never you mind."

Precious shrugged and went upstairs to check the lights on each doorjamb so she knew which woman was available when the customers came in. Goddess' light was red, which wasn't surprising, she was a busy woman, but what did surprise her was the fact she was at work at this time. Precious shrugged again. Maybe the woman had taken on extra hours. As Precious didn't actually care, she returned downstairs and walked into the living room, all smiles.

It was time to get flirting.

Chapter Ten

The days since they'd been little seemed ages ago, locked in a time when the lenses kids saw things through were laced with innocence and their souls hadn't been corrupted. Precious and Boycie had continued to do whatever Everett said—and it was getting worse, the way he ordered them about. He'd turned more spiteful when they were about eight.

Secretly, Precious wished she could stand in his shoes, be the one telling everyone what to do, but he'd been in the role for too long and would never give it up. He'd been strange for years now, never discussing his home life, always changing the subject if she brought it up. She had a feeling it wasn't exactly a stable life he lived, but that was only going by her gut instinct—and the fact that again, since they were eight, no one had been allowed to go round to play in his street. Boycie had told her to leave it, to not ask questions. To be honest, Precious didn't give much of a shit except for the fact that whatever was going on affected Everett's mood. Oh, and he'd taken to calling himself Roach but wouldn't say why.

The years of primary school were behind them, and at secondary it was a lot harder to misbehave and avoid consequences. Roach told her to bully this girl or that boy, but she'd started telling him to do it himself. What was his obsession with it anyway? She should ask herself the same question. What was her *obsession? Why had she always, as far back as she could remember, picked on people? Why couldn't she pick on Roach? Why was he different?*

There was just something about him that told her not to bother. He got a look in his eyes sometimes and it could be quite cruel, but she still believed he'd make them rich one day. He'd promised. To make some pocket money, he bought cans of Coke for cheap down the corner shop, loaded them into his rucksack, and sold them for a pound each at school. He never shared the profits, even when Precious and Boycie helped flog them, he just walked off with the coins jingling in his pockets.

But the thing he did that bugged her the most was sometimes he talked to Boycie off to one side, leaving her out. Was it because she was a girl? Or didn't they want her in the gang anymore and hadn't got around to telling her that? Maybe she should jump before she was pushed.

The past few months she'd been pissed off at being cast aside sometimes, their whispers and side glances getting on her nerves. She had her eye on some mean girls who paraded around the school like they owned it. She could teach them a thing or two about being nasty. They weren't quite at top-tier level yet, but neither were they the kind to welcome her into their group just like that. She'd probably have to work for it. Or be bold and tell them she was joining them, giving them no choice; but to do that she'd have to gather evidence. Secrets. Things she could bribe them with. No one wanted hidden sins spoken about, especially not teenage girls.

So instead of hanging around with Roach and Boycie, pacing up and down the school field at lunchtime selling Cokes, she'd been walking around by herself, listening to conversations, inserting herself into them and even bringing up certain subjects regarding the three girls she had her eye on. Sasha, Tanya, and Lucy were all pretty. All had faces full of makeup, and all smelled of expensive perfume. Precious had plenty of makeup and perfume, her mum and dad weren't poor, but those three seemed on another level financially. Still, she could fake it and fit in well enough. She'd always felt superior to most of the kids at school anyway. Loads of them had parents on benefits.

It made her wonder why Roach sold the cans of Coke. She hadn't been given the impression that his family was skint. But then as he hadn't discussed them, she had nothing to base her judgement on. Were they secretly poor like Samuel and he needed to make money in order for them to eat? Talking of Samuel, he'd moved to Lincoln to live with an aunt because his mother had topped herself. Mum had mentioned it in passing, saying it was tragic. Precious hadn't given a toss. As long as things didn't affect her, she didn't much care. Apparently, she was like her great-aunt

Sarah, the word selfish *bandied about whenever the woman was discussed.*

Again, Precious didn't give a toss.

A group of girls sat under a tree in the corner of the school field. They ate their packed lunches while talking. Precious sidled behind them and settled on a bench next to a large tree trunk. They were so engrossed in conversation they didn't take any notice of her.

"That Tanya's a right fucking bitch," one of them said.

"Why, what's she done now?"

"She's only gone and thieved Melissa's bracelet, the one that's got her dad's ashes in it."

"Bloody creepy, carrying ashes around."

"That's not the point, that bracelet's too important for Tanya to be playing around with it."

"What's Melissa done about it?"

"Nothing. She's too scared of her."

Precious got up and found the trio in the other corner of the field, trying to hide a KFC they must have nipped out to collect. The red on the bucket gave the game away.

Sasha eyed Precious warily. "What do you want?"

"I heard Tanya stole Melissa's bracelet. The one with the dead dust in it."

Sasha smirked. "So what if she did?"

"Is that all that's going to happen? It's stolen and you're not going to do anything with it?"

Tanya placed her hand on her bag, over a pocket where the bracelet probably hid. "To be honest, I don't think it's got fuck all to do with you."

"No, it hasn't, but I thought it would be funny to torment her with it. What's the point in having it if you're not going to do sod all? So far, all you've done is make her cry about her poor dead daddy. You've missed the opportunity to really fuck her up."

Lucy didn't seem to like the idea of taking it further. "I think it's pretty shitty enough to just take the bracelet, don't you?"

"Oh, are you feeling sorry for her?" Precious asked. "Have you got a conscience or something? You won't get very far with one of those."

Lucy plucked a blade of grass and fiddled with it. "Yeah, well, there's being a bitch then there's being a bitch. We've all agreed that making her cry was enough."

"Why did you even pick her?" Precious asked.

"Because she was rude to us last week," Tanya said.

Precious had an idea that that was probably because last week was the father's funeral and Melissa was understandably testy. "What are you going to do, give it back to her?"

"Eventually."

"What are the ashes in?"

"There's like a moonstone on it, and you unscrew it; the ashes are underneath."

"Then tip them out in front of her and give her the bracelet back. That would seriously fuck with her head." *That was a bit too far even for Precious, and she didn't even know where the idea had come from. It happened like that a lot, where ideas formed and she acted on them. Mum reckon she needed to see a therapist or something, but sod that. Precious didn't want anyone poking around in her brain, thanks. She didn't understand it herself, so how could anyone else? Besides, those therapists just pretended to listen and got paid loads of money for it.*

"That's really mean," Tanya said. "I like it. The trouble is, we risk getting in the shit with the headmaster for that. May even get suspended."

"You can't be that hard then if you're worried about something like that." *Precious jabbed a hand on her hip, goading them.* "I thought you were supposed to be tough, the toughest girls in the school. Doesn't sound like it to me."

"You go and tip the ashes out in front of her then," Sasha said, "if you think you're harder."

"Give me the bracelet." Precious held a hand out.

Tanya took it from her bag and placed it on Precious' palm. The moonstone gem was quite big, about the width of a penny, and she reckoned she'd get some ashes on her fingers, which would be gross. But she wasn't even going to do that. This was her way inside the trio's gang, and she only had to give the illusion that she was harder than them. She just had to get a bit threatening with Melissa, that was all.

"Back in a minute." She walked off to find her.

She spotted her sitting on a bench, alone, with her back to the playground. She faced the wire fence and the bushes beyond, staring into space. To be fair, she looked wrecked, and Precious should leave it a week or two before she did this, but she wanted to be part of the gang more than she wanted to give Melissa time to grieve.

"I got your bracelet back off Tanya. Before I can give it to you, you need to promise me something."

Melissa's eyes filled with hope. "What is it?"

"If anyone asks, you've got to tell them I tipped the ashes out."

Melissa gasped. "Please don't do that..."

"I'm not going to, you silly bitch, you just have to make out I did."

"Why do I even need to do that?"

"Because I said so." She fished the bracelet out and pretended to unscrew the moonstone just in case anyone was watching and saw her arms moving. She shook them for good measure, as if tipping out the ashes, then passed the bracelet to Melissa. *"Oh, and one more thing. If rumours spread and a teacher asks whether I emptied the ashes, you say I didn't."*

Melissa gripped the bracelet and frowned. "I don't understand."

"You don't have to. Now pretend to cry or I'll actually punch you to make you."

Melissa bent her head.

Precious got up and strutted back over to the gang of girls. "That's how you upset someone. If you need any more lessons, just ask me."

"You can sit with us if you like," Sasha said.

Really? It was as easy as that?

For once, Precious felt like the leader instead of the follower. If she could get these bitches to do whatever she said, she'd be the equivalent of Everett, holding all the power.

It would be good to be in charge.

Chapter Eleven

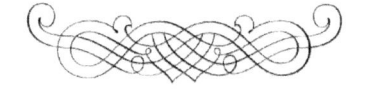

Cooper stared at Kayla. He couldn't compute what he was seeing. She lay on her side on the bench—that position couldn't be comfortable. She gazed ahead at the pavement, her hair spotted red. He shifted his sights to her chest to see where the blood was coming from. A gaping gash in her neck. He'd sent his runners off not twenty seconds ago to fulfil the orders that had come in, and now he wished he hadn't. Standing here alone, with the killer possibly hiding in the tree line, wasn't something he should be thinking about, first and foremost. His sympathy should be with Kayla, but fear had crept in.

He swore he was being watched from the darkness. The trees looked so ominous; someone could be hiding from behind any one of those trunks. Despite that, he turned away from her to scan the street. No one waited around for drugs, and all the curtains were closed. He spun back to stare at her again, stepping forward a few paces, then taking one step at a time, slowly, as if she'd jump up and scare him any minute and say it was a joke.

But even he knew this was no joke. She wouldn't have gone this far just to get a laugh out of him.

"Kayla?" he whispered urgently.

She didn't reply, of course she didn't, but the hope she would gripped hold of him. He slid his phone out of his pocket. Who should he ring, the police or The Brothers? But what if the *twins* had sent someone to kill her? What if they'd found out she'd helped to murder Alice? And if he phoned the police, they'd ask him what they were doing there. Yes, he had the twins' protection, but he couldn't exactly tell the coppers that, could he, because then they'd know he was up to something dodgy by selling drugs.

He stood about two metres away from her. Some of the blood had got on her black puffa jacket. Some had dripped off onto the bench slat. It then dribbled down onto the grass. There was no way the twins could cover this up in time, not in a residential street. But then someone had crept up behind her and slashed her throat in a residential street, and they were nowhere to be seen, so could George and Greg do the same if they came to collect her?

He opted to ring Boycie. There was no way that man could cover this up either, but if Cooper could just get some words of advice, that would help to stem his panic. He dialled him on the burner. The ringing stopped abruptly, and he stalled on what to say.

"I'm at Skein Road. Kayla's had her throat slashed. Some fucker must have come up behind her and done it while I was busy."

"You what?"

"I said—"

"Yeah, I know what you fucking said, I was just trying to get my head around it. Has anyone seen anything? The neighbours, I mean?"

"How do I bloody know? Anyone could have been looking out of their windows."

"Shit, you're going to have to ring the police, no one can cover this up. You'll have to say you were meeting her there, and when you got there, you found her like that. You'd better pray no neighbours spotted anything going on. They could have already called the police anyway. Ring The Brothers and let them know you've called the plod."

"Right, okay."

"Also, when you get home, switch off then destroy any burner phones that were used for the Alice thing. They should have been got rid of ages ago, but if for some fucked-up reason she decided to keep hers… You don't want any incriminating evidence hanging around."

"Right."

Cooper prodded the END CALL button. He looked at Kayla again. Fucking hell, he couldn't believe she was dead. Would the twins admit they'd sent someone to do it? He stabbed their icon in his contact list and waited for them to answer.

"Having problems with the skagheads?" George asked.

"I wish. Someone's killed Kayla in Skein Road."

"You'd better be fucking me about, son."

"I swear to God, I was talking to the runners, and then when I turned around she was dead. They must have been hiding in the trees. I don't know if any of the neighbours have seen anything either. Boycie said I ought to get hold of you and then ring the police."

"Yeah, I'll get hold of our copper. He'll likely be the one to come out to the scene anyway. What's your story?"

Cooper repeated what Boycie had told him to say.

"That might work so long as no one witnessed anything."

"Was it you two?" Cooper asked.

"What would we want to kill *her* for? Granted, there's no love lost between us, and as far as I know, she hasn't fucked us over, so she was free and clear. Do you know something we don't by any chance?"

"God, no. It's just she told me about that time she lied about that bloke in the pub, saying he'd touched her up. I wondered if it was about that."

"That was sorted ages ago. Old news. But someone's got a beef, so you'd better watch your back. Get on and phone the police. Let me know what's going on later."

Cooper stared at his phone screen. There was time to get upset later, but for now, and even though it sounded bad, he had to cover his arse at the minute. Distance himself from any wrongdoing. Make himself out to be a good boy—because if plod found out he was a dealer, he'd get arrested.

Grateful he didn't have any gear on him, the runners had taken it, he forced himself to calm down. He glanced at the bench again and finally saw her as his girlfriend, not a very dead problem that needed to go away. Fuck, he'd really liked Kayla, thought they'd be together forever.

She'd said she was being followed, and he'd brushed it off. God, what a wanker. And what George had said floated through his mind. *You'd better watch your back.*

Jesus Christ. What if someone came for *him* next?

Chapter Twelve

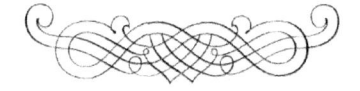

Quite frankly, Boycie knew damn well it was Precious who'd done this. A fucking big coincidence if it wasn't. He'd waited a few minutes before he phoned the twins, but he couldn't put it off any longer.

He got the sense that things had been unravelling ever since Roach's murder. He hadn't realised how much Roach had taken charge until he had to do it himself. Making all the final decisions had turned out to be harder than he'd expected.

He'd bet Precious was all smug now. Fucking hell, why couldn't she have just waited? And she had some brass balls on her to murder someone opposite a row of houses. All right, it was dark near the trees, but still. He hadn't rung her; he was too angry.

He dialled the twins' number. When George answered, he said, "Has Cooper phoned you yet?"

"Yep."

"Do you think it could be to do with drugs? Had she maybe bragged about her boyfriend selling them and someone killed her, thinking she'd have some on her? She was at Skein Road, so she must have gone out to sell with him."

"I agree, it could have just been a random druggie who took too much and it skewed their brain. We need to go as we're on an observation job at the minute and have to be ready to at a moment's notice. Message later if there's any developments we need to know about. Bloody hell, this means we're going to have to go and pay

Kayla's parents a visit to offer them help with the funeral. That's another thing on our to-do list. Anyway, we've got to go, catch you later."

Boycie paced Precious' living room. She'd done this behind his back. And hadn't she talked about going after Edna tonight? She couldn't kill two people in such a short space of time, he wouldn't let her. He went into the hallway and put his coat and shoes on, then walked out and headed in the direction of the Orange Lantern. He'd stand outside all night and wait for her to leave. March her home so she couldn't do a detour to Edna's. They needed a bloody good chat, and he wasn't going to let her fob him off anymore. She'd gone against their plan, and he wasn't sure what to do about it. Precious was too much of a live wire for him to try to tame her. Next thing he knew, she'd suggest Cooper ought to cop it an' all.

What the fuck am I going to do about her?

Chapter Thirteen

In their taxi across the road from their warehouse, George had already contacted Bennett about the CCTV. The bloke wasn't on duty at the moment, but his colleague, John, was. As he was also paid by the twins, John had turned the camera to point away so nothing was picked up. His excuse, should anyone ask, would be he thought he'd seen someone lurking in the bushes down the way, and then he got distracted by another screen and forgot to switch the camera back to point at the warehouses.

Men had been dropped off in taxis. They'd spoken to a big fella on the door, showing him some ID, presumably, and then were allowed inside. Only a few stragglers had arrived in the past hour, and George had estimated about seventy men had entered the property so far. The big man still stood on the door, and if George wasn't mistaken, he was packing a gun. It created a telltale bulge under his suit jacket. The weather had turned a bit nippy lately, so if the bloke was going to be standing there all night, he'd soon get cold.

This warehouse wasn't the same as the twins' who had iron railings and a gate, padlocked so no one could get near the front door. This one had more of an open-plan frontage, and seven cars were parked. He assumed they belonged to the sex workers. The Bains' SUV was there, too.

"What the fuck time is this party going to end?" George muttered.

"God knows, but we'd have been better off getting Ichabod or someone else to do surveillance instead. I don't see the point in sitting here for another few hours when we know damn well Farah and Joseph are probably going to leave here and go straight home. Why don't we get someone here to watch then follow, and put someone else outside their house so we can be told when they've arrived. We'll nab them from their place. It'll be easier because the location's out of the way."

George glanced at the time on his phone. It was getting on a bit, but Greg had a point. They could be eating in the Noodle instead of sitting here twiddling their thumbs. Now he'd thought about food, George's stomach rumbled. "Let's go and get some dinner."

"The usual place?"

"Yep."

Greg drove away, and George messaged John to let him know they were no longer there, then he organised for someone to sit at the warehouse and outside the Bains' gaff.

"What do you think about this Kayla bullshit, then?" George asked.

"Well, she's clearly pissed someone off, hasn't she? Cooper doesn't strike me as the kind of bloke who'd do that to her and then cover it up."

"No, maybe it's like Boycie said and it was a random druggie. What gets me, though, is that if she sat on that bench by those trees, he was too far away from her to have got to her in time, even if he'd seen what was going on. When someone's got it in their head to slit your throat, nothing's going to stop them, is it? Even if he'd shouted at them, they'd have done it anyway."

Greg sniffed. "All the same, we need to find out who did it."

"Like anyone's going to talk around there. Skein Road is full of no-hopers and those who like to keep secrets. The majority of them would even turn their nose up at fifty quid for grassing. They'd want a grand, the greedy bastards."

Greg sighed. "We'll wait for the police presence to die down and then go to the street and question people. Surely someone, if they saw something, could be persuaded to let us know. If it has to be a grand, then it has to be a grand. Not that I'm too pleased that we're having to do this for a girl we couldn't stand."

"But she was a resident all the same."

"Yeah. We'll do right by her. Unless, of course, we find out she's been into some dodgy shit and she was killed because of that. To be honest, I thought it was weird that Vicky Hart just happened to stay with her before she fucked off to Essex, if that's even where she went. It's obvious to us now that the name was just used as a disguise. What if Kayla knew? What if this fake Vicky murdered her? What if Kayla lied to us, making out she didn't know anything about Alice's death?"

"Then we should have a word with Cooper. Put some pressure on him, see if he crumbles. Especially because he'll be upset about Kayla dying. It's easier to get the truth out of someone when they're grieving."

"You're a wicked bastard, but I suppose if it gets the job done…"

Greg turned into the Noodle car park and drove into a slot. They got out and entered the pub the back way. Nessa caught sight of them and held up a hand, gesturing to let them know she had something to tell them. She was busy serving someone at the minute, so George and Greg stood at the bar and waited. A few seconds later, she mentioned a woman called Edna would be coming in tomorrow morning to do some baking to see if her cakes were good enough to sell.

"Hang on a minute," George said. "An *Edna* doing *baking*?" He looked at Greg. "Am I having a déjà vu or what?"

"It certainly seems off," Greg said.

"What are you on about?" Nessa asked.

George pinched his chin. "We'll pay a little visit while she's here. I think she's been telling us a few porkies."

Nessa frowned. "Shit, is she someone we shouldn't be employing? Because I'm happy enough to sack her off and tell her not to bother turning up."

"No, we definitely want her to come here." George shook his head at Greg. "I fucking *knew* she was odd and something wasn't right with that setup."

"Yeah, we got caught up with the fact that names were being borrowed, and we assumed hers was, too. But there's no way she's *our* Edna. This bird isn't old, for a start, when our cook was."

They ordered dinner and a Coke each, sitting at a table in the corner. George opted for a chicken and mushroom Pot Noodle with tiger bread, and Greg picked chicken and chips. Just as the food arrived and they were about to tuck in, someone walked in, and it had George's eyebrows hiking up.

"You might want to look over there," he said.

Greg glanced at the bar where the woman now stood. "Ah, bollocks."

"Let her come to you," George advised. "It's obvious she's here to see if this is where you are. It just so happens that we've proved her right, which is a bit of a bummer for you."

Ineke glanced over and caught them staring. She didn't look too happy, but then Greg had said she'd been complaining about being left alone a lot. She approached the table but remained standing.

Greg looked up at her and smiled. "Everything all right?"

"You told me this morning that you'd be back by six. We were supposed to be going out, but obviously I'm not important enough for you to have remembered that. That's fine, I'm used to broken promises." She held a hand up to stop Greg from explaining himself. "This isn't a pity party and me trying to make you feel sorry for me." She sat and leaned towards him but stared at George. "There's three people in this relationship, and I think it's time we called it a day, don't you?" She eyed Greg. "I'm not your priority, he is, and yes, you told me that from the start, but I didn't think it would be this bad. If I'm allowed to stay in the flat, as we agreed when I first came to England, that would be lovely, but if you'd rather I didn't, then I'll pack up and find somewhere else to go."

"Stay where you are," Greg said, sounding detached. "We wouldn't go back on the flat offer, nor the jobs, nor your uni course. Everything can stay the same, except us two."

George nudged Greg's knee under the table. His brother was being a bit too blasé about this, showing hardly any emotion. Maybe that was because Ineke had chosen to break up with him in public, and even though she was being quiet, it was still a humiliation should someone overhear. Greg wouldn't want anyone to know he was gutted, although he probably wasn't, considering he was going to finish with her anyway. But there would still be feelings of attachment, the memories of the fun they'd had, and how close they'd got so quickly.

"We'll still be friends?" Greg asked.

"Of course." She stood and smiled down at him sadly. "Thank you, though, for trying. I should never have tried to come between you, I see that now. I was warned that if I pushed you too far, you'd back off completely." She glanced at George.

He recalled that conversation. "I'll be as blunt as usual: it's a shame you didn't listen to me then, isn't it? Still, we can all be mates, no need for anyone to get shitty—or spiteful, is there?" He meant it as a warning and was pleased to see she'd taken it as such. He glared at her: *If you leak any of our business, I'll fucking come for you. If you tell anyone about the murders in Amsterdam, I'll fucking murder you, too.*

She blushed a little, and he should feel a bastard for scaring her, but she was on their turf now, and she had to understand the rules. Just because she'd had a crap upbringing, it didn't mean she had a free pass on the Cardigan Estate to act however she wanted.

"I'll be off then," she said. "See you when I see you."

She walked out, and George expected Greg to go after her, but he didn't.

"Do you know something I don't?" George asked.

"What do you mean?"

"Well, I thought you'd have at least given her a cuddle or something. You've let her walk out, probably crying her eyes out by now, and feeling alone."

"I know her well enough that she'd want to be left by herself to process it. I'm not going to push myself on her when she doesn't need me around at the minute. She realised I wasn't going to do what she wanted, I wasn't going to be told what to do, and she needs stability, not somebody who barely comes home." Greg shrugged. "We thought it would work and it didn't, end of."

He continued his dinner as if the conversation hadn't taken place. George was a master at hiding his feelings, but fucking hell, Greg won the gold medal today.

George dipped tiger bread in his Pot Noodle sauce and got on with the business of eating. It didn't feel right to discuss the breakup in front of customers, and he had a feeling Greg needed a moment to process it by himself. Despite him wanting to split from Ineke, it would probably come as a shock that she'd wanted the same thing and had got in there first.

They finished their meals and sat back, Greg taking his phone out and switching it on. He stared at the top corner of his message icon, a white number seventeen inside a red circle. George assumed they were all from Ineke.

"Did you completely forget you were supposed to take her out?" George asked.

"Unfortunately, yes."

"Then she *definitely* wasn't the woman for you, because if she was, you'd never have left her sitting there at home alone, waiting, you'd have at least said something had come up and we were busy."

"I feel like such a selfish cunt. I should have cared more, but you and the Estate mean more to me than she does."

"At least you can be honest about it. I wonder how she'll get along now. I hope this doesn't set her back. We don't need more drama on our hands."

"She's stronger than you give her credit for. Look what she survived in Amsterdam. She picked herself up and sorted herself out. We've given her the means to do that with the uni course, the cheap rent, and paying her to work for us. I'm sure I'll have to face her at some point so she can get everything off her chest, but for now,

I'll read her messages to see how much shit's likely to come my way."

Greg opened up the message string, scanned them, and frowned. "It's not as bad as I thought. She's quite calm, saying she realised a job had come up tonight but could I at least let her know whether I'd be coming home this evening. Then a bit later she says that I clearly haven't even looked at my phone because none of the messages are on 'read'. Then the last one is she'll see me whenever, just before she walked in here."

"You got away lightly," George said. "No screaming and carrying on. Then again, look at who you are, who I am. She's hardly likely to go off on one, is she?"

"I don't think she's scared of me, not anymore. She knows I wouldn't hurt her unless she really fucked us over."

"Then you need to make *sure* she's scared of you."

Greg sighed again. "I'm not looking forward to the chat, but I know it's got to be done. I do owe her an apology. I've been funny with her ever since she started picking on you behind your back. I should have told her from the minute I knew it wasn't going to work."

"But you didn't want to hurt her any more than she already had been."

"I know, but that doesn't mean that was the right thing to do."

They sipped their Cokes, George feeling a bit guilty that he was pleased Ineke had ended things. He'd had the niggles with her ever since he'd found out what she'd been saying. And even if she'd stayed with Greg, it would never have been the same. George would never have seen her as a sister-in-law. She'd just be the annoying woman he disliked. Maybe this way they *could* still be friends.

Chapter Fourteen

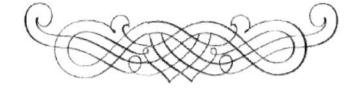

Goddess sat on the sofa in the safe house, Will on a chair opposite. He told her a bit about why he worked for the twins and how they'd helped him. It was clear he was one of their biggest fans. She was beginning to see that they weren't the monsters the rumours said they were. It sounded as if they had hearts of gold underneath their mean exteriors. Will predicted they'd kill Farah and Joseph just to get them out of the way. The fact they ran sex parties at the warehouse wouldn't go down too well. As they hadn't asked for permission either, that was another black mark against them.

Goddess grappled with her conscience. She shouldn't want anyone to be killed, but Farah and Joseph wouldn't think twice about killing *her* if she continued to refuse to do what they wanted. Joseph had bragged that he'd killed a woman before, and she didn't want to be in the same boat as his victim. Maybe he'd only said that to frighten her into obeying, but she couldn't take the risk. Sleep had been hard to come by. She'd woken every couple of hours, convinced Joseph would break into her house and kill her—or the other person would.

It was so odd, because when she'd started at their escort agency, they'd been nice to her, emphasising that sex was off the table and if any man approached her for it, she had to tell Joseph. Maybe they did that to all the women to lure them into a false sense of security. Had they asked others to work at a warehouse? They must have done. Had any of them refused and they were going through what Goddess had?

"Will the twins make sure the other women are okay?" she asked.

"Yes, they'll have already found out who they are, where they live, and new jobs will be lined up for them. Debbie, who runs the parlour at The Angel, she'll find them work. She also runs the women in Kitchen Street. If there are too many new girls, she might even set up another spot."

Happy that George and Greg seemed to have all angles covered, she relaxed a bit. Would she owe them now? Would they expect her to do something for them in return? She dreaded to think what that might be, so instead of dwelling on it, she picked up a pack of cards from the coffee table and took them out to shuffle them.

"I take it you don't mind playing to pass the time," she said.

"Go Fish?" He smiled. "I used to play it as a kid."

She dealt the cards, trying to remember the rules of the game. Giving up, she asked Will to remind her. He explained, and they played a few games. Goddess was surprised she even had it in her to laugh, and it felt good to be safe and do something so normal. Considering what might be going on right now, she ought to be crying, but Will had a way about him that put her at ease.

Her mind wandered. The party at the warehouse would be in full swing. Were the twins going to barge in there or wait until it was over? She wished they'd told her what they were going to do so she wouldn't be so nervous, imagining different scenarios.

"Do you think they'll wait until Farah and Joseph leave the warehouse?" she asked, unable to keep her thoughts to herself.

"Probably," he said. "They're not going to want anyone to know it was them who killed them. They'll likely just make them disappear, if you catch my drift."

"Where will they put the bodies?"

"It's best you don't know anything like that. They wouldn't be happy with me telling you anyway. If they want you to know, they'll tell you."

He was right, it *was* best she didn't know. She'd only have nightmares in the future, seeing them dumping the bodies, but her mind didn't want to play ball, and it showed her Farah and Joseph being buried in a remote place.

Oh God. "Will they make me do anything to pay them back?"

"I doubt it very much. You haven't done anything wrong. And to be honest, you telling them what's been happening has done them a favour. They employ people to tell them shit like this, but clearly stuff goes on without anyone knowing about it. George gets angry about that, when secrets have been kept, and I think he finds it difficult to cope with the fact that they don't know everything. He loves being in control, so to not have any does his nut in."

"How can they be on top of it all when their Estate is so big? People do things behind closed doors all the time." *Like me.*

"True, but try telling George that. He'll beat himself about it, like he always does. All he wants is a safe Estate for their residents. When crap like this keeps going on, it pisses him off. I wouldn't want to be in Farah's and Joseph's shoes, he won't go easy on them."

"I thought they'd just get told off for not paying protection money." *I thought their business would be closed down, as per the plan.*

Will laughed. "It isn't just that, though, is it? You're one of their residents, and they couldn't protect you until you stepped forward. It'll annoy them that you've been threatened. It'll be okay, George will get over it, but at the moment I expect he's so angry he can't see straight."

"You said they're like brothers to you. How many people feel that way? They must have helped loads."

"I expect hundreds of people look at them differently now. Did you know that George has envelopes full of money in his pocket all the time and if he sees someone skint, he helps them out? The amount of times he's handed cash over so people can put their electric on is unreal. He really does care." He paused. "Is there anyone associated with Farah and Joseph that they need to know about? What I mean is, is there anyone who'd come after you for them once it's clear they've gone missing?"

"No, it's just them." *But there is someone else who'd come after me, only I'm not allowed to say. The stakes are too high there...*

"Good. I was going to say that if there was a problem, the twins would likely put you in one of their flats until everyone was rounded up. They own a fair few."

"Is that so it looks like they've got a legitimate income with the rents?"

"I'm not going to answer yes or no on that one because it's their business. I have to warn you that with you asking so many questions, I'm going to have to tell them. For all I know, you could be trying to find information out for someone to be used against them."

"I'd never do that." *I would if I had to.* "Forget I asked anything."

"You'll be watched afterwards, you know. They'll be looking to see whether you're dodgy or not. They've trusted people who've shafted them afterwards. Fair warning, if you mess them about, you'll end up dead, too."

They'll watch me? Shit! "I gathered that. I just want to get on with my life. With Farah and Joseph gone, I'll be able to do that." *Liar.* "They've been scaring me for too long now."

They played some more Go Fish, then Will got up and made cups of tea. He bought some biscuits in on a plate, and they munched on them in silence.

Goddess wouldn't be able to sleep until she knew it was over—*all* of it, not just this crap. She leaned back on the sofa and stared at the ceiling, imagining what could be going on now. She had no idea how long the warehouse parties went on, so she guessed she was in for a long night, but the party wasn't the only thing she wondered about. There happened to be someone else who relied on her to do the right thing. If she didn't, it was game over.

Chapter Fifteen

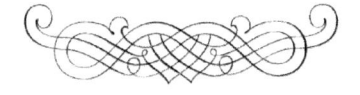

School had come and gone, and at eighteen, Precious couldn't be happier. No more rules. No more homework. And as for exams, they could fuck right off—all done and dusted, although she hadn't fared too well. She had a job in a crappy little shop which didn't please the parents too much. Mum had thought she'd "do better", be a secretary or something. Precious was

always disappointing them, not only in her behaviour but her achievements, or lack thereof.

What happened to your life being yours when you hit eighteen? What happened to choosing your own destiny? Since when, once you became an adult, did you still have to do what your parents wanted? She supposed if she brought it up, Mum would give her the speech about living under their roof and only paying minimal rent. Well, that could be sorted—as soon as Precious could move out, she would.

But she'd forget all that for tonight. It was Friday, and that meant party time. She was going clubbing. She often wondered what it would be like to go out with Boycie or Roach. She hadn't seen them for ages. After she'd ditched the mean girl gang, finding once again she didn't have any control at all, she'd kind of drifted through the last stages of school. She'd occasionally hung out with Boycie and Roach, but the sale of cans of Coke had turned into white-powder coke, and while she was a rebel, she really didn't want to be kicked out of school for being involved.

Where the fuck Roach got that stuff from she didn't know, but she'd heard he was selling in the clubs now, although she'd never seen him in one. She'd also heard he rented his own flat, so he must be making quite a bit of money. He'd always said he'd be rich. She missed them, or specifically, how life used to be, when there had been less worries and responsibilities. She'd spent all that time longing to grow up so she could do whatever she wanted, but she'd found that wasn't the case at all. Dad had told a little fib there because grown-ups had to follow the rules, too. That was a bit of a shit. But being older, she'd worked out how to skirt round some of them and even to break one or two.

Tonight she was going out with the ginger girl neighbour who'd come knocking in a minute so they could get the bus into town. She was well aware she was a user. As a five year old, she'd ditched Ginger Susie when she'd found Boycie and Roach more interesting, then she'd picked Susie back up every time she had no one to hang around with. Susie didn't mind, she was just grateful that Precious had anything to do with her at all.

The doorbell rang, so with one quick glance in the full-length mirror to see if she looked all right—she did—she went downstairs in her Doc Martens. Mum had already opened the door and spoke to Susie on the doorstep, giving her the unnecessary lecture about keeping safe and making sure nobody put drugs in their drinks. Precious rolled her eyes and stepped outside, looping arms with Susie as they walked down the street.

Sometimes she got a bit nostalgic, memories from the past assaulting her out of the blue. Playing out on this road. Skipping on the pavement. Knocking on people's doors and running away. Stealing the apples from the old lady's garden. Telling Mrs Courson to fuck off over and over again.

"What are you smiling at?" Susie asked.

"This bloody street and what we used to get up to. We had some good times, didn't we?"

"We did. You used to be so naughty, though. You didn't give a single shit about getting in trouble. I don't get it because your mum and dad are really decent people."

"You're lucky I don't take offence at that, you cheeky cow. Yeah, they brought me up right, but I just couldn't behave. Mind you, Dad did encourage me to play up sometimes. I think he wished I was a boy. I bet if I was, it would've been more acceptable for me to stick my fingers up at people."

"Wonder why that is?"

"What?"

"Why you can't behave, because you're still like it now."

Precious shrugged. "Fuck knows, and who even cares? Come on, the bus is here."

She tugged Susie along, and the double-decker wheezed to a stop. She made sure they jumped to the front of the queue, even though several others had been waiting. A middle-aged couple gave her a dirty look, but she threw them one right back.

"We all get on in the end, so what does it matter what order it is?" she said. "Christ, get a life." She shook her head at them, then led Susie down the aisle.

They sat at the back on the lower deck, Susie's cheeks bright red. The couple glared in Precious' direction as they found some seats, so she raised her middle finger. If memory served, she'd pissed them off as a child, too. It seemed they weren't in the mood to put up with her when they were in their fifties either. God, some people had a rod up their backside, didn't they?

The bus lurched off, and the man of the pair had to grip the pole to stop himself falling as he hadn't sat yet. Precious burst out laughing so he knew she'd seen him. He blushed and quickly sat.

"You're so rotten," Susie whispered.

"Fuck 'em. I seriously couldn't care less."

It didn't take long to get to town. They walked down the high street towards Dance Fusion, a new club that had opened last month. There was already a queue, even though it didn't open till nine o'clock. It was only seven now.

"Fuck waiting there like a spanner," she said. "Let's go to the Red Lion."

The pub was packed, and that bloody awful-looking woman sang in the corner. The posters advertising her 'act' said her name was Lil. As for her clothes…

Precious pushed through the customers to the bar, getting a few filthy glares while she was at it. Lil wailed 'I Will Survive', and women, drunk or not, sang with her. Precious tried to drown out their voices and shouted her order: two large glasses of white wine. She paid and handed Susie her glass, then they went to a relatively empty corner. There were no seats, standing room only. It would probably empty out here after nine o'clock, although saying that, going by the looks of some of these people, they weren't the type to go to Dance Fusion — too old and past it.

They had two more drinks, then weaved their way back down the street to tag on to the end of the queue for the club. Susie got chatting to a friend of hers, so Precious people-watched, picking fault with each person she clapped eyes on. The street was busy with people either going to the kebab shop, the pizza restaurant, or the pub. She got jostled a few times by folks walking past on the way to the Red Lion. Some rules weren't meant to be broken, but shouting out while in the queue was one she had to follow if she wanted to get inside. Anyone being rowdy in the line was refused entry, and if she had to go home and spend the rest of the evening bored out of her mind, she'd scream.

Eventually, they reached the head of the queue. As usual, because Precious had only just turned eighteen, she had to provide ID here. No other place asked her for it. She rolled her eyes and produced her driving licence. The bouncer let them in, and as they didn't have thick coats on, they didn't bother queuing for the cloakroom. They headed straight for the dance area inside a massive horseshoe-shaped bar made of transparent plastic, its innards filled with piping lit in neon colours, very industrial meets sci-fi. People were already dancing, the disco lights flickering on and off. Red, green, blue, orange, then startling white in strobes.

It was Susie's turn to buy drinks, and even though Mum's advice was boring, they followed it. Susie ordered alcopops so they could put their thumbs over the tops of the bottles in between sips. They danced for a bit, had two more bottles, and then Precious got the shock of her life.

It shouldn't have been a shock, not really, but she hadn't expected to see them here—and wasn't that stupid, since she'd heard Roach sold drugs in clubs? He and Boycie came towards her, both of them smiling. She stepped forward for a three-way hug, Susie forgotten, and followed them to a corner where they could at least hear themselves speak. They caught up for around an hour, then Roach asked her if she needed a job. It involved selling drugs. She shrugged, not giving a shit so long as it made her money. She agreed to meet them tomorrow for lunch so they could discuss things. Then they disappeared on her. Had they left the club? She found Susie who'd copped off with a fella and didn't seem to want Precious butting in.

That was all right, she could find the bloke of her own. She shifted between the dancers until she spotted someone attractive. For some reason he wasn't interested in her, and she had the urge to poke his eye out with her thumb. She moved on to the next man who looked about five years older than her. He was drunk off his face, which didn't bode well in the dick-hardening department, so she gave up and danced on her own instead.

A couple of hours later, she'd had enough and went to find Susie who sat on some other bloke's lap. She looked like she'd had too much alcohol, her head lolling to one side.

"Have you fucking spiked her drink?" Precious shouted, then stared at him in shock. "Oh my God, Samuel?"

He frowned at her as if he didn't remember who she was.

Then I'll have pleasure in reminding him. *"Remember me? I nicked your sandwich when we were five. Miss Taylor made me say sorry, but I wasn't then and I'm not now."*

Recognition and then hurt flitted across his face. Was he contemplating whether to have a go at her or not? "Is this your mate?"

"Yeah."

"Then can you do something with her, please? She just came over to me and sat on my lap. I don't even know her. She's off her face on something, probably drugs."

"Can you help me get her outside at least?" A bit of a big ask, not to mention rude, considering the sandwich thing and how she'd just spoken to him, but oh well.

He nodded, and with one of Susie's arms over each of their shoulders, they half dragged her to the door. Samuel didn't step outside, he left Precious to it.

Luckily, a lit taxi came by, and she managed to stagger towards it.

Fucking hell, remind me not to go out with her again.

<hr>

Precious met her childhood friends in the Dog and Gun on the Moon Estate. She hadn't needed to ask why. It would be dodgy to talk about drugs on Cardigan, too many ears listening an' all that. But being on Moon didn't mean they were safe either. According to the rumours, there were spies everywhere. Roach had already solved the eavesdropper issue by passing her a sheet of A4 paper. He'd typed everything he didn't want to say out loud, and while he and Boycie browsed the menu, she digested whether she wanted to get involved or not.

Unlike when Roach sold the apples and cans of Coke, she'd at least get paid this time. One rule was that under no circumstances would they be out on the streets showing their faces while they were peddling. Roach and Boycie wore bandanas or mouth masks over the bottom halves and sunglasses over the tops. Roach was pretty chuffed that no one knew who he was beneath his disguise—he even went so far as to change his voice while acting a gangster. According to the sheet of paper, he bought the drugs and distributed them to his runners, and Boycie was his right-hand man. So what would she be? A lowly runner? She wasn't too happy at being cut out yet again, lesser than they were, but she'd keep her mouth shut for now, because the weekly payment offer at the bottom of the page was too much for her to turn down.

"What do you think then?" Roach said. "And are you up for a bit of argy-bargy from time to time?"

"What do you mean by argy-bargy? Giving someone a slap?"

He huffed out a laugh. "And the rest."

She was unsure what he meant by that, but it wasn't exactly something she could ask about in public, was it?

He handed her a pen. "Ask any questions on the other side of the paper and I'll answer them."

They went back and forth a few times, and, satisfied with the terms—apart from the last one, but she'd just have to cope with it—she nodded. If he asked her to beat someone up, she had to do it. If he asked her to threaten someone, she had to do that, too. And if he asked her to kill someone... She'd imagined doing it but hadn't thought she ever would. She supposed in that line of work there would be people who took the piss, owing

Roach money. And maybe death was what they deserved.

She glanced down at the questions and answers.

What does "and the rest" mean?
Killing. Slitting throats, shit like that.

How much would you pay me for that?
A few grand.

Be more specific.
Three.

And that's on top of my weekly wage?
Yep. You'll be better off leaving your current job. You'll be working at night for me and will need to sleep in the day.

I want all of this in writing.

Don't you trust me?

I need somewhere else to live. Nosy Parents.
You can doss at my flat. Move in tomorrow if you want.

How much?
Rent-free, plus extras when I want them.

She hadn't bothered asking what extras meant, his grin had been answer enough. That was fine, seeing as she didn't have a fella at the minute, but she'd have to speak to him about when she did. Would he still expect her to put out if she had a boyfriend?

She caught Boycie reading the Q&A session. He narrowed his eyes and seemed pissed off. What did he care if she gave Roach extras? It wasn't like Boycie had ever said he fancied her or anything. God, they were just friends—so that might make it awkward to have sex with Roach.

Then again, for free rent and those wages, she'd probably do anything.

Chapter Sixteen

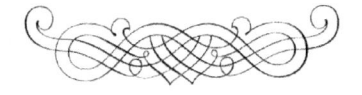

Colin was on his first proper job for the twins. Janine had warned him he'd have to steer investigations in another direction. There was a time he'd never have done this, but losing his wife had turned his brain somehow. He'd lost his compass that sent him in the right direction, and now all he wanted to do was get justice in any way he could. How on earth had he morphed into someone he'd once despised? He didn't even care if he got caught. His life was lonely now, no one to come home to, no one to nag him that he was spending too much time at work.

Janine had been a godsend, and he'd gone round there for dinner plenty of times. She'd come to the funeral and held his hand the whole way through, even though she had a tiny baby at home. There had been a month's delay in the release of the body, the police holding on to it for evidence. Her boyfriend, Cameron, had looked after the little girl who they'd named Rosie. Colin couldn't wish for a better friend and pillar of support. And there was him at one time thinking she was a moody cow. She still was, but she was *his* moody cow, and dare he say it, he'd grown really fond of her. He understood her more since she'd explained why she'd gone to work for the twins. He had the same burning urge to right the wrongs in any way he could, and if that meant doing it on the dodgy side of the law, then that's what he'd do.

He had a few meals in the Taj with the twins, in a back room where no one could see him. He hadn't even felt bad striding through the rear door to join them in secret. He carried a smouldering rage inside him all the time; he was afraid if he didn't let it consume him, he'd think about his wife and how awful it had been to find her dead. How awful it must have been for her to know she was going to die, and before that, raped. She was a good woman and hadn't deserved that, and God forgive him, but if working for the twins and being perpetually angry helped him to put that to the back of his mind, then he'd do it.

The house wasn't the same with her gone. Everything seemed so cold and bland—and quiet without her laughter. She'd had a dirty laugh, he'd always told her that. And he missed her cooking. He'd realised, too late, that those meals had brought him comfort after a long, hard day, and she'd chosen them on purpose so he'd relax quicker. She'd thought about him a lot, he'd discovered, again too late, even down to putting cans of Pepsi Max in a fabric cool bag for him to take to work with him. He'd always found them on the side by the kettle where she must have put them before she'd gone to bed.

He'd taken her for granted and hated himself for it.

Surprisingly, his DI, Nigel, someone Colin couldn't stand when he'd first started working with him, had also turned into a godsend. He'd gone easy on Colin when he'd returned to work, plus had done his best to try and find the killer, but sadly, the bastard was in the wind. He'd used a condom, and none of his DNA had been left behind, so he was either forensic savvy or fucking lucky. No fingerprints, fuck all in the house to pin anything on him. It was enough to send Colin into a murderous rage himself.

Why my wife? Why did it have to be her?

He stared at the dead woman on the bench. Why had *she* been killed? Was she an innocent person, too, apart from making up lies and fibbing to the twins about some bloke in the pub touching her up when he hadn't? She hadn't deserved a slit throat for that, but then again, she could have caused problems for other men and one of them had waited patiently until they could teach her a lesson.

The gash in her neck revolted him, so he turned away for a moment to scan the tree line. Whoever had killed her could have come and gone from there. Unless it was a resident who'd nipped across the road, did the business, then went home again. Unfortunately, her boyfriend, Cooper, had arrived here and found her already dead. He'd said the street had been empty when he'd got here. He'd walked across the grass towards the bench, thinking she just lay on her side for a rest or something, even though he knew that was stupid thought. His mind hadn't gone to her being dead. When he'd reached her and seen her neck, he'd nearly been sick.

The bloke seemed to be telling the truth. He looked too shocked to be lying. Colin had been a copper for a long time and prided himself in spotting who was bullshitting and who wasn't. It wasn't hard to put himself in Cooper's shoes; after all, he'd found the woman he loved dead, too.

"Maybe someone mistook her for a skaghead," Nigel said. "I mean, this bench is known for drug addicts to zone out on. We could have some nutter going around topping addicts. The CCTV around here is shite, so I don't anticipate getting any footage that will be any good to us, unless they walked through the trees to the left and came out by the shops."

"They wouldn't be that stupid, would they?"

"I don't think so, I'm just putting it out there. Door-to-door enquiries hasn't provided anything. Nobody saw a bloody thing."

"That's not unusual for this street. Everyone's tight-lipped."

"What, even if there's a murder on their doorstep? Even if one of their neighbours did it?"

"*Especially* if one of their neighbours did it. They won't want to grass and get a slit throat themselves."

Nigel shook his head. "It doesn't make sense. You think they'd want the fucker off the street, not living right next door to them."

"Maybe they're all sick of the skagheads coming round here so they've turned a blind eye. Who fucking knows with this lot." Colin had to watch himself; he'd sounded apathetic then, like he didn't give a toss who'd done it. But he had to. He had to discover who it was so he could tell the twins. His apathy was more directed at people who could stand idly by and not say a word. He'd never understood that in the whole time he'd been a police officer. But hang on, wasn't *he* now one of those people? Someone who turned the other way?

"You sound tired, Colin."

He snapped out of his head and smiled at Nigel, albeit a wan one. "I'm all right, I actually slept last night for once."

Nigel folded his arms. "I didn't mean that kind of tired."

Since he'd become a widower, he'd found his patience was at an all-time low. "What *did* you mean?"

"Tired of the rat race. Tired of us continually chasing people who do bad things."

I'll be doing bad things now. "Yeah, well, it gets you down sometimes."

"And you miss working with Janine." Nigel smiled. "It's all right, you can say so. I know exactly what it feels like to have your senior officer disappear on you."

"She didn't disappear. She had a baby."

"You know what I meant."

"Sorry. I just get a bit snappy more than usual lately."

"Understandable."

"It's just he's out there and could be raping someone else, know what I mean?"

"We did everything we could, you know that. I'll find him in the end, and maybe it'll give you some measure of peace when I do. I know it'll never bring the missus back, but at least we'd have got justice for her."

"I appreciate it." *But if I find the fucker, I'll be killing him, not bringing him into the station.*

Nigel turned to glance at the street. Jim, the pathologist, had arrived. Colin knew the twins hadn't killed this woman on the bench, but he was a tad nervous about what direction he was supposed to send the case in. They hadn't told him what they expected him to do.

He remembered what Janine used to get up to and gave Nigel a gentle nudge with his elbow. "I just need a break for a minute. Won't be long."

He walked off towards the edge of the pavement and found a space where no other officers stood. He clocked a lot of neighbours in their front gardens, all of them being nosy. And who could blame them? It wasn't often a body sat on a bench in direct view of your lounge. It was likely the most exciting thing that had happened around here in ages.

The tent hadn't gone up yet, but it would shortly—Sheila Sutton, the lead SOCO, had arrived with her team. Colin shuffled along a little more to get some privacy, then turned his back on the scene and took his burner phone out, the one he used to contact the twins. He'd already ensured his ringtone and message bleeps were turned off, only the vibrate on. He sent a message.

COLIN: WHAT AM I SUPPOSED TO BE DOING?

GG: MAKING IT LOOK LIKE A DRUGGIE BUMPED HER OFF.

COLIN: FINE. WON'T BE TOO HARD, NIGEL'S ALREADY LEANING THAT WAY. WHAT ABOUT THE BOYFRIEND?

GG: HE'S NO ONE TO BE CONCERNED WITH.

COLIN: OKAY.

He popped the phone in his pocket and turned to walk over the grass. The tent was being erected, and onlookers craned their necks to get a good gander. Had the neighbours in his street done the same on the night Colin's wife had been murdered? He couldn't remember now, it was all a blur. He peered over at where Cooper stood with two PCs. The poor sod looked wrecked.

Colin went to stand next to Nigel again. "I've had a think, and I reckon you're right. Someone's bumped her off thinking she was off her tits on coke. Maybe they even thought she had drugs or money on her so they killed her to steal it. Plenty of desperate bastards in this area."

"Yep, it seems clear enough to me."

They waited until the tent had completely gone up, and as they were already in forensic outfits, they followed Jim inside. The photographer joined them, taking several pictures while they all stood and watched. This had happened at Colin's house. His colleagues had done exactly the same there, only they'd had more empathy because it was his wife. Jim got on with doing his initial checks, and when he'd finished, he rose from his knees and sighed.

"The cut was made with the person standing at her back. I doubt very much she even heard them coming. The slice is clean, no jagged edges, therefore she didn't struggle, unless she was held still. When I do the post-mortem, I'll swab for fibres in and around her mouth in case she was gagged to keep her from screaming." He stared over at the houses. "One of the uniforms said nobody saw anything. Un-bloody-believable."

Sheila poked her head inside the tent. "Is it okay if I come in?"

Jim nodded. "We thankfully don't need to disturb her to look for ID. Her boyfriend turned up and found her here. Her name's Kayla Barnes."

"Which reminds me," Nigel said, "we need to go and visit her parents. Cooper's already given me their address."

George had said he and Greg would be going there tomorrow. Colin didn't know much about what they did behind the scenes, but apparently they'd be giving the mum and dad money to help with the funeral, something they did a lot with other people. How did they feel handing money over, knowing they'd sometimes been the cause of the loved one's death? He supposed they'd have to pretend to care, even though the scum they'd killed had deserved it.

"Shall we go then?" Colin asked.

They left the tent and took off their forensic gear in a cordoned-off space, placed the items in a bag, signed the log, and left the scene.

Nigel drove through the streets, frowning. "How do you tell parents that you suspect their daughter was a case of mistaken identity or she was a target without sounding like you don't know your arse from your elbow?"

"Maybe don't say that until we know for sure. Something might come to light in the next few hours or tomorrow which will change our whole perspective."

"True. There's no point in upsetting them if we don't have to. It's bad enough that she was murdered at all. Do you recognise her name?"

Colin's gut lurched. "No."

"I've got Chris looking into her back at the station, but maybe the parents will give us some insight into who she was, providing they feel up to it."

"It'll be a bit of a bugger if they had no idea their daughter was hanging around Skein Road."

"It'll be a shock an' all. Going by their address, they appear to be respectable people. Cooper said he's never met them, reckons they wouldn't approve of him. Apparently, Kayla told him they were a bit iffy about who she hung around with."

"That'll be him getting the blame for this then. Not that he killed her, but that they were meeting at the bench in such a dodgy place, and if Kayla hadn't been seeing him, none of this would have happened, et cetera."

"He seemed a nice enough bloke to me. The poor sod's in bits." Nigel tutted. "Sorry, that was insensitive of me. Of *course* he's in fucking bits."

There had been a few times Nigel had corrected himself lately, and it might end up being a problem. Colin wasn't going to brush it under the rug this time.

"Look, is it awkward working with me knowing that my wife got killed? Do you feel you have to watch what you're saying? Because if it's going to make things weird between us, I can always move departments." *I don't want to because the twins need me on the murder team, but...*

"I *do* worry that I'll put my foot in it, but there's no need for you to go elsewhere. We've got used to each other now, and to be honest, I don't want to have to make friends with another DS. You were exhausting enough at the start with your barriers as high as the bloody Shard."

Colin smiled. He *had* been a bit of an arse. "Fine. I'm here to do a job, and it's going to involve similar things to what happened to my missus. I have to accept that and get on with it. You need to act like it's just another crime, regardless of my feelings."

"Okay. Did you make a decision about whether to retire or not? Like I said, getting to know another DS… Selfish of me, but would you consider staying?"

"Already considered it." *And I can't exactly fuck off now the twins need me.* "Besides, what the hell would I do all day at home without her? Work will stop me from going mental. It'll stop me thinking."

"Good."

Nigel pulled up to the kerb and parked behind a silver Audi. The house was in a better part of the Cardigan Estate, a detached red-brick in a row of five. Despite it being late, the living room light was on, one of the curtains partially open. Through the slice, Colin spied a man sitting on the sofa, reading what looked like a Kindle. A woman sat at the other end watching telly. They were about to walk in there and ruin their whole lives. Colin wished he could sit in the car for a bit longer so the couple could remain oblivious. Would the dad ever finish that book? Would he be able to stand going back to it, knowing the exact sentence he'd stopped at when he'd heard the doorbell?

"I don't want to do this, but we have to," Colin said.

"I'll lead, but jump in if the fancy takes you. I appreciate it's going to be tough on you."

They left the car and walked up the garden path. The woman glanced out and caught sight of them. She frowned, clearly wondering what the hell two men were doing on her path at this time of night. She spoke to the man, and he got up to answer the door before they'd even knocked.

"Yes?" he asked.

Nigel held up his ID and gave him their names. "James Barnes, isn't it?"

"Yes… What do you want?"

"We're here about your daughter, Kayla."

"Oh God, what's she done?"

"It's best we come in." Nigel smiled tightly.

James stepped back and gestured for them to go into the living room. Colin followed Nigel in there and stood awkwardly by the door as James went over to sit by his wife who was in the process of turning the television volume down.

"Karen?" Nigel asked.

"Yes. What she been up to? I knew the day would come when we had the police at our door. Who's she upset this time?"

James seemed embarrassed by her outburst, as though he didn't want anyone to know that they were aware their daughter might be a wrong 'un. "Please, take a seat. Would you like a drink?"

"No, thank you." Nigel sat on the armchair, looking a bit stiff. He obviously hated this part of the job.

Colin remained by the door, unwilling to step up to the plate and save the DI. Not that he was being an arsehole, but he had to observe, pick up on any clues the parents might give away. Something he could use to steer the case towards it *definitely* being a druggie who'd killed Kayla.

Nigel took a deep breath. "It's with regret that I have to inform you that Kayla died this evening. She's already been identified by her boyfriend."

Karen stared at them, her mouth hanging open.

James blinked. "W-what? How? Was she poorly?"

Nigel appeared even stiffer, and he formed a double fist which he hung between his open knees. He squeezed rhythmically, then: "I'm afraid it was murder."

"Oh my God!" Karen shrieked. She stood and did a strange little dance, as if she couldn't work out if she needed to run from the room or pace. She opted to flop back into her seat. "Did she upset someone that much that they came after her?" She looked at her husband. "Didn't I *say* she'd piss off the wrong person? Didn't I *warn* her she couldn't keep going around telling lies about people?"

Colin didn't think the shock had hit her yet, or maybe her mind was protecting her by concentrating on Kayla's behaviour so she didn't have to face what she'd been told.

James cleared his throat. "What did she do? She must have upset someone if this is how they've retaliated."

Nigel unclenched his hands and rubbed his knees. "She may not have done anything. She was sitting on a bench in Skein Road, waiting for her boyfriend. As far as we know, someone approached her from behind. She may not have known they were there until it was too late."

James closed his eyes. "What did they do to her?"

Nigel glanced at Colin, as though asking whether he should reveal it yet or not—as in: *Can they handle the drama tonight?* Colin nodded. They were better off having the full truth now rather than the shock of it later.

"She had a cut to the throat," Nigel said.

Karen let out a wail. "Would it have been quick? Would she have been in pain?"

Again, Nigel looked at Colin.

"Only for a second or two," Colin lied. He had to make this easier for them—he knew exactly what hell they'd go through. If he could ease it a bit, they'd have fewer questions swirling in their heads in the middle of the night. "The amount of blood loss, and so quickly...she would have likely passed out." Jim would probably correct him on that one, but for now, it would help to lessen the parents' burden. "I realise you probably don't want to answer any questions, but it's very important that we learn as much information about Kayla as possible so we can find who did this to her. You mentioned she's upset people in the past. Do you know who they are?"

"Honestly, there's too many to mention," Karen said with a touch of disgust in her voice. "There was her up the road. Her in the next street. People in the pub. She has a habit of being spiteful for the sake of it, almost like she enjoys it. I've never understood it, and she wasn't brought up to behave that way. We've got to the point where we don't see her much anymore. She says we expect too much of her, and *I* say all we expect is for her to act like a nice human being. I can only imagine what type of man her boyfriend is. She loves winding us up, so she's probably chosen somebody on the wrong side of the law."

"I feel bad even saying this," James said, "but my wife's right. Kayla can be nasty, even to us, and she *likes* hurting people. There must be a long list of who could have done this to her. She finally messed with the wrong person…" He'd said that last bit as if to himself. "But I'm not pleased about it, of course I'm not, I'm devastated, but I'm sad to say it doesn't surprise me. Not that I expected someone to murder her, but I *did* expect her to come here one day with a broken nose and a bruised face. There's only so much people should put up with, and she pushes too many buttons. But we loved her anyway, we always will. I wish this hadn't happened and I wish she'd listened to us, but she had a will of her own and thought we were trying to stifle her."

"There are a lot of kids like it these days," Karen said. "Entitled, the lot of them. They think they can gad about doing whatever they want. Half of them don't even care about the consequences."

"Would you say you're estranged?" Nigel asked.

"Not really," James said. "We're here if she needs us, but sadly, she doesn't. Or didn't. Where is she now?"

Nigel winced. "I'm afraid she's still on the bench where she was found. There's a tent covering her, but she'll remain in situ for some time while forensic work is carried out around her."

"How long will she be there for?" Karen prodded the off button on the remote control. "What I mean is, when can we see her?"

"At some point tomorrow," Nigel said. "You can phone the station, and someone will get in touch with the pathologist to arrange for you to go down there."

At Karen's grimace, Colin interrupted—she was more than likely imagining her daughter with a gaping slit in her neck. "She'll have a sheet up to her chin. You'll just see her face. You can say goodbye in private."

He'd done that himself, telling his wife how sorry he was that he hadn't been home that night. That him going to see Janine about work had seemed more important, yet again, than her. He'd said he wished he could turn the clock back, and that he'd listened to her and retired earlier than he'd originally planned, but he'd wanted the full pension—another thing he'd ignored her on. If he hadn't done that, she'd probably still be alive. But then was that true? Did every soul have a specific amount of time on the earth, and when it was up, it was up? Would she have died that day anyway, even if he'd stayed at home?

Nigel chatted to them for a bit longer. Colin found the parents' practical, realist natures disarming. It was as if all emotions had been switched off except for blaming their daughter for putting herself in the position to get murdered. Maybe Kayla had had a point after all, and she'd distanced herself from her parents because of their attitude. Maybe their expectations of her were too high and she'd railed against it.

With everything covered and Kayla's work address written down, they said their goodbyes and left. The Barnes couple didn't want a family liaison officer, nor did they want to talk to anybody about what had happened, so a therapist was off the table. Karen wanted to be left alone to digest the shame of her daughter hanging around in terrible streets where she didn't belong—her words.

Maybe one day they'd realise that no matter what their daughter had done, she still hadn't deserved to die like that.

Or had she?

Chapter Seventeen

The call came that there was movement at the warehouse. Greg parked the taxi round the corner out of the way of any cameras, and in their disguises, they walked to sit inside the back of Ichabod's stolen car opposite the building.

"As ye can see, all the cars have gone bar the black SUV," Ichabod said. "A shedload of customers left the buildin', and then some women, which I assumed were staff. Unless the SUV owners are takin' someone else home, then I'd say only your targets are inside. I take it the CCTV camera was moved so that I'm not seen?"

"Yeah, John did it, so don't worry. How long ago did the last person leave?"

"About twenty minutes."

"Shit, so there could be a lot of cleaning up to do yet. We might have to settle in for the duration."

Ichabod stared across the road. "If the cameras have been turned away, aren't we better off waitin' down the side of their warehouse in the dark?"

George nodded. "That's not a bad idea. Let me just double-check with John first."

GG: Cameras still pointing away from warehouses?

John: Yes.

GG: Keep it that way until you're told otherwise.

George popped his phone in his pocket. "Come on, then."

They left the car and trooped over the road, veering right down the darkest side of the warehouse, closest to the SUV. George left Greg and Ichabod near the front and went for a prowl around the rear. All of this row of warehouses backed onto the Thames, somewhere the twins used to dump chopped-up bodies. George had missed his circular saw as they'd opted to work in the cottage recently.

The back door had a padlock on the outside, which was a fire risk. George went to stand with the other two and whispered to them about the padlock.

"At least we know they're not goin' tae exit that way and catch us here," Ichabod whispered back.

A clonk from the front of the building had them all stiffening, then came a creak and footsteps with high heels tapping.

"God, that's got cold out here," a woman said.

George peered around the edge of the building. That had to be Farah, dressed to the nines in designer gear. The bloke she was with wasn't short of a bob or two either if his suit was anything to go by. The pair of them must make a lot of money, but then seeing their house had hinted at as much.

She trotted over to the SUV, heading for the driver's side, her husband opting for the back for some reason. George ran out into the open and launched himself at Joseph. Farah stared over at Ichabod and Greg pouring out from the side of the warehouse. An abrupt scream shot from her mouth, and then she turned to run towards the road. Ichabod reached her before she got anywhere near the pavement. He hauled her across the street to his stolen car, a forearm arm across her throat.

"What the fuck?" Joseph said.

"You're coming for a little ride with us." George gripped the bloke's arm tight. "Now we can do this the easy way or the hard way, it's entirely up to you. If you fancy mucking me about, go ahead, but it won't end well for you, but if you want to be a civilised gentleman, then walk with me to our taxi parked around the corner."

"Who are you?" Joseph looked between George and Greg, then back to George. He seemed genuinely confused as to who they were—not surprising because of their disguises—but also regarding what they were doing, bursting into his life like this. "What do you want?"

"You'll realise who we are when I tell you that we want protection money for your businesses that you failed to tell us about. You've got a right little sex den going, haven't you? Then there's that escort agency you run. What I don't like the thought of is you threatening women to work for you. If a woman says no, she means no; that doesn't just apply to sex, it applies to all aspects of life. One of the ladies who used to work with you moved on elsewhere, and you and your wife decided that would be a good idea to badger her and try to get her to do shit in your warehouse. She said she didn't want to, but you kept on. What gives you the right to think you can get away with that?"

"You're talking about Goddess."

Does that mean, if they know it's her, that they haven't been putting pressure on any of the others? Why just her? Or did she complain the loudest, so he assumes it was Goddess? "Glad to see we're on the same page. Right, well, we'd best be off. We've got a lot to do tonight, and fannying about here talking isn't going to get us anywhere."

Greg took Joseph's other arm, and they marched him across the street and around the corner to the taxi. George decided to do one of his old tricks and use bungee cords to secure the bloke in the back seat. He shoved a cloth in Joseph's mouth, muffling his protests, then clipped another bungee cord into hooks in the boot. The cord lay across the material and held the gag in place, tugging on Joseph's head so it tilted back. The bloke kept trying to talk, even though it was pointless. George took no notice and got in the passenger seat, reaching into the glove box for a lemon sherbet for himself and Greg. They sucked on them all the way to the cottage.

"Ichabod's following but has stayed a good way back," Greg said. "I can't see Farah."

George laughed. "He's probably folded her up in the boot."

Greg stopped outside the cottage, and with a twin on each side of the taxi, they undid the bungee cords. George let Greg take Joseph inside while he waited for Ichabod to park.

The Irishman opened his car door and got out. "I had tae do a sleeper hold on her so she went unconscious. She was going tae be trouble otherwise. She was gettin' all mouthy, and it got on my nerves."

"Fair enough. Let's get her inside."

Ichabod opened the boot, and George reached in to pick her up, throwing her over his shoulder. She was light, so it didn't take much effort to walk her inside. Ichabod had already secured her wrists behind her back with a cable tie, plus her ankles. George put her in the corner so if she woke up, she'd see the back of her husband, who'd soon be hanging from the hooks in the ceiling. At the moment, he lay on the floor with a bleeding mouth. Greg must've punched him and knocked him over. He'd planted a foot on the bloke's throat to keep him still. One extra-hard press and his Adam's apple would be wrecked.

"Please just let us go and we'll close the businesses," he said, his voice raspy.

"It's too late for that, sunshine." George walked across to loom over him. "Not only did you keep a lot of protection money from us, you've threatened one of our residents. I realise you're residents, too, and quite the swanky house you've got an' all, but you lost your privileges the minute you started on Goddess."

"Please…"

"Save it. Did you think she wouldn't have the guts to get some help? Were you not aware that you can only push people so far before they snap?

You were an absolute cunt to her, and you're going to have to pay for it." He turned to Ichabod. "Shut the door, will you, mate? Lock it and pop the key in your pocket for now in case that silly cow wakes up and tries to hop away."

Ichabod followed the instructions and moved to stand behind Joseph and hold his waist. Greg held Joseph's arms up, and George clipped the manacles around his wrists. Ichabod wandered away to stand against the wall by the door. George went over to the handle on the wall and turned it so the chains lifted their captive. He kept going until the man's feet were half a foot off the floor.

George nodded at Greg, and at the same time, they took knives out of their pockets and cut at Joseph's clothes, removing them. Greg opened the trap door and kicked the material scraps into the gap. Joseph had remained quiet throughout, clearly the type of man who dealt with issues in silence. Or maybe he knew that protesting wouldn't get him anywhere. He'd been caught out, and there would be no going back.

"Please let Farah go," he said. "She wouldn't have done any of this if I hadn't forced her into it."

"So you're trying to tell us that your wife's innocent, that she didn't threaten Goddess."

"Yeah, she did, but only because I made her do it. I threatened my wife, too. She knows if she doesn't obey, I'll hurt her."

"I don't believe you."

George unravelled the garden hose from the wall and switched the tap on. The power-washer attachment on the end spurted water in a violent line, and he aimed it into the corner at Farah. It hit her with force, denting her skin, and she woke up screaming, gasping for air at the shock of the cold liquid. George turned the stream at Joseph's arse, firing a hard shot of water between the wanker's cheeks, just because he could. Joseph cried out, his knees shooting upwards, his balls shrivelling. George put the hose back and walked over to Farah. He grabbed the top of her arm and wrenched her to her feet, dragging her to stand in front of her husband.

"This is the predicament you find yourselves in when you don't follow the rules," he told her. "I expect you wish you'd come clean about your businesses now. You'd have only lost a bit of money each week, but now you're going to lose your lives. Where's the cash from this evening's little sexual jolly?"

"She had a handbag," Ichabod said. "I'll go and get it. It's in the footwell."

George nodded and turned his attention back to Farah. "We're going to take that money as payment for what you owe us, although I imagine you owe us a damn sight more because you've been running your escort agency for a good couple of years, haven't you? Are we going to find cash at your house, because I can't see you being able to put much of that in the bank without the taxman asking questions. Is it in a safe? Or have you gone old school and it's in shoeboxes under the bed?"

"It's...it's in a safe."

"And what would be the combination number for that?"

"If I give it to you, will you let us go?"

George glanced across a Greg. "Can you believe the cheek of her? She actually thinks she can bargain with us. I don't think she's quite got the gist." He swung his attention back to Farah. "Give me the fucking number or I'll cut your tits off." *I think I'm going to do that anyway.*

She shrieked at him, panic sending her chest up and down quickly. "Oh God, please, please don't hurt me."

"I'll do what I fucking like, thank you, seeing as though I run the Estate with my brother. *You* answer to *us*, not the other way around. So, what's that number?"

"Two, five, two, five."

"Thank you—see how polite I can be, even when cunts like you piss me off? You'll understand why I'll send someone into your gaff now to make sure you're not lying to me. If you are, it means whatever I do to you will hurt more."

"It's the right number, I swear."

Joseph shook his head as if he couldn't believe they were in this position. "There's about eighty grand in that safe. Take the lot."

"Oh, it wasn't up for debate. I intend to take it without your permission, like you set up two businesses without ours." George took his phone out and sent a message to one of their men, telling him to break into the back of the house and get that safe open.

GG: TAKE FIVE GRAND OF THE MONEY FOR YOURSELF, THEN DELIVER THE REST TO THE NOODLE.

I know it's late, but knock Nessa up and give it to her. Tell her to put it in the safe, in a bag away from any of the pub money.

He slipped his phone away. "Right then, let's get down to business." He smiled at Farah. "You're going to stand here and watch your dear husband get his nuts and cock chopped off. Then I'm going to shove that cock in your mouth and tape your lips shut."

Ichabod came back in and held the handbag up. George gestured for him to put it on the table, then he carried her a few steps away and positioned her back against the wall. He bent down to snip the cable tie at her ankles, then stood next to her and rested a hand on her stomach to keep her in place. They had a bird's-eye view of Joseph's tackle. Greg went to the table in the corner and selected a small pair of pruning clippers. He returned to Joseph and stood to the side of him, grasping the end of his foreskin, pulling and elongating the dick. He positioned the blades at the base and cut. Sharp as those blades may be, it still looked like he had to use some force to squeeze the handles together.

Blood pissed out, and he casually walked around the back of the man to stand on his other side so he could snip that, too. He dropped the cock on the floor and attacked the bollocks in the same way. Joseph could no longer hold his silence. He screamed, the wound at his groin losing so much blood it dribbled down his inner thighs. Farah let out a quiet sob.

"I bet that's really hurting him," George said to her. "And you'll find out how much when we lop your tits off. It'll be painful, because we'll snip, snip, snip, all the way around, cutting open the skin, then slicing into the flesh using a hacksaw. You might wonder why I've chosen your private parts, but they represent sex and everything you've done wrong regarding that, so they seem as good a thing to torture you with as any. I don't even know why I'm explaining it to you. Maybe I want you to shit yourself because you know what's coming. Maybe I want you to imagine it before it actually happens so I can watch the humiliation as piss drips down your legs." He glanced at Joseph. "He's finally shut up then."

Joseph had passed out.

Greg put the shears back on the table and picked up a sword, something George had been using a lot lately. Greg drove the tip into the base of Joseph's neck, right out of the back. He withdrew it then sliced across. Scarlet flowed out in a sheet down Joseph's chest, creeping lower to meet the mess at his groin. Farah turned her head to the left so she wouldn't have to see, but George gripped the front of her clothes and dragged her forward a bit, standing behind her and holding her forehead steady under his palm so she had no choice but to watch. With two fingers of his other hand, he held her top eyelids open.

"You don't get to close these unless I say so. You don't get to do anything unless I say so. Unless, of course, you piss yourself—that's an involuntary action in these sorts of scary circumstances." He laughed in her ear. "Can you see the way his body's twitching, the last of his life flickering through his body? Some people don't believe the rumours about me and my brother. I don't think they can handle the fact that someone could be so wicked. I expect that's what you two thought. Otherwise, there's no way you'd have not paid that protection money. You probably thought this day would never come. And maybe it wouldn't have if it wasn't for Goddess. But that's your fault, for pushing the woman too far until she couldn't stand any more. You've only got yourselves to blame."

Greg swung the sword upwards and chopped clean through one of Joseph's wrists, then the other. Joseph fell through the trapdoor hole, the thud of his body landing somewhat muffled by Farah's screams. Greg picked the cock up and stuffed in her mouth.

"Shut it, you noisy bitch." He went to the table and collected the duct tape, biting a long strip off.

George kept Farah's head still and forced her mouth closed with his finger under her chin. She choked on the dick, but neither of them took any notice of her. Greg taped her mouth closed, and together, without needing to say a word, they removed the cable tie around her wrists, took Joseph's hands from the manacles, then put Farah's in their place.

"Who wants the first snip of her tit?" George asked and roared with laughter.

Chapter Eighteen

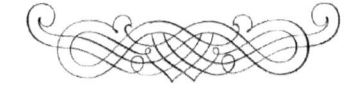

Being a runner wasn't so bad. The best part was hiding her hair beneath a beanie and covering her face, people not having a clue who she was—it gave her a sense of power. She sold to some of her old neighbours, and they had no idea she was the one passing them coke and weed. Mum would have a right fit if she knew some of the residents were secret

druggies. It was amusing, watching these people quickly get into their cars, rushing off down the street, likely paranoid the police were lurking nearby to arrest them.

That was the part of the job Precious disliked the most, keeping her eye out for undercover coppers or even those in uniform. It distracted her from her main job, where she also had to keep a lookout for people who wanted to rob her. The first one who'd done that had lost the use of his legs for six weeks. She'd punched him to the ground then jumped on his shins with both Doc-Marten-encased feet, creating fractures. She and Boycie had dragged him into the bushes in someone's garden and left him there, passed out.

Living at Roach's flat was way better than being at home, although he was similar to Mum in that he asked her questions. Where did you go? Who were you with? What have you been up to? She didn't feel she needed to answer any of them, so didn't, telling him to mind his own fucking business and laughing. She could tell he hadn't liked it, but just because she lived with him and worked for him, it didn't mean he had the right to know every little detail about her life.

She hadn't told Mum and Dad her address, just that she'd moved in with a mate. She'd told them it was a girl call Jasmine, and no matter how many times

Mum asked where it was, Precious didn't relent and tell her. At this rate, if Mum kept on, Precious wouldn't be going round there anymore. It was becoming a chore to do the Sunday visit, especially after being awake until five in the morning from selling on a Saturday night. She often fell asleep on their sofa after dinner, then Dad offered to take her home, probably so he could find out her address. But she always walked to the end of the street and phoned for a taxi. If they knew she could afford one of those, they'd ask if she'd got a pay rise, and she just couldn't be arsed to explain that she no longer worked in that crappy shop. As it was, Mum had already asked where she was because she hadn't seen her in there recently, and Precious had made out she'd been moved to another branch and worked out the back sorting the deliveries. The amount of lies she told was unreal.

It was Friday night and, in her bedroom, dressed all in black, her bandana and sunglasses in her pocket, she stuffed her hair in a top bun and hid it under her dark woolly hat. Roach was in the kitchen, drumming his fingertips on the worktop, something that really annoyed her. She was sure he did it on purpose. It was his way of telling her to hurry the fuck up. They were meeting Boycie in Reginald Street to drop a bag of drugs to him, which he'd hand over to the runner there, keeping watch as it was a rough-as-arseholes area. Then Roach was taking her to Leopold Road, her latest haunt.

She switched off her personal phone and popped it in her bedside drawer, locking it and hiding the key under her rug. Roach had never snooped in here as far as she was aware, but she still liked the semblance of privacy.

They left the flat with their faces uncovered and got into Roach's car. He changed number plates frequently and once a month paid someone to respray the car completely. He never bothered letting the DVLA know. She didn't much care what he did, so long as she never got caught inside it.

He didn't speak on the way to Reginald Street, and she got the sense he had more than his business on his mind. Boycie had mentioned Roach's dad the other day, saying he'd seen him in the Co-op. Roach's expression had shown his anger, and Boycie had asked him what was wrong.

"Don't talk to me about that bloke," Roach had snapped, and that had been the end of it.

Clearly, he'd fallen out with his old man, and if she could be bothered, she'd tell Dad about it to see if he could find out any gossip. But she couldn't be bothered, she didn't care enough, and anyway, Roach had turned back into his normal self an hour or two later.

Halfway there, he instructed her to cover her face, pulling up to the kerb so he could hide his. Then he continued driving and stopped next to Boycie. He reached into the back seat for one of the large bumbags and passed it out of the window.

"Everything shipshape?" he asked.

Boycie looked menacing with his face hidden. "If it wasn't, I would have phoned."

Precious waited for Roach to bark at him for being rude, but he didn't. He must be in a good mood tonight. He nodded at Boycie, hit the button to wind the window up, and continued on to Leopold Road.

She reached into the back for her bumbag, clipped it on, and got out. She stood beyond the light of a streetlamp, hiding in the shadows within easy access of an alley that led to a park which had four exits. A great way to confuse the police if they ever chased her. Roach drove away, then the druggies poured out of the darkness as if they'd been waiting for her to arrive and for Roach to piss off.

She sold a fair bit in the first half an hour, then there was a lull, which gave her time to think about which direction she was going in life. She didn't want to stay a runner forever. She wanted to move up in Roach's business, to earn the same amount of money as Boycie did. Although admittedly, he did a damn sight more than her. He was the intimidator, the one who threatened the customers. He spread the word that Roach was someone not to be messed with, said that if anyone crossed him, they'd end up dead. She could well imagine Roach getting his hands dirty, but now he had her, why buy a dog and bark yourself? She'd be the one killing now, not him.

With her bag half-empty an hour later, she frowned at her phone ringing. The only people with this number were Roach and Boycie, and neither of them ever called her if they could help it, they sent messages. She took it out of her pocket and glanced at the screen. Roach. Something serious must have gone down.

She answered it but didn't speak, just in case someone had nicked his phone off him or it was the police.

"It's okay, it's me," he said. "Come to Reginald Street, we've got a bit of a problem and only you can sort it out. Someone's taken too long to pay me."

Her first reaction was a sinking heart at the thought of jogging all the way across the park to get there, but then excitement took over. "All right. Give me a couple of minutes."

Someone cruised by in a car, the bloke who bought several wraps at a time, so she did the exchange with him and began her jog through the park. She pushed on between some trees and came out to stop at the edge of a green that parted the two sides of Reginald. From here she could observe the street. No one was around. A grunt from behind had her spinning round, her hand on her pocket that contained her flick-knife. She quickly withdrew it and released the blade, staring into the darkness that had trees as a backdrop.

"It's just us," Roach whispered.

She relaxed and stepped forward. "Where are you?"

"Over here."

She'd gathered that, but where? She followed where she thought his voice had come from, finding him behind a tree trunk in the woodland that bordered the park beyond. She personally thought it would be easier to deal from here rather than in the actual street, but Roach always shot down any of her suggestions as if she didn't know what she was talking about. She supposed he was right in that they'd need torches to check if the right amount of money was being handed over, but other than that, she thought it was a good idea.

"Come on, we'll go over there," he said.

She followed his shape, plus a couple of others—presumably Boycie and the druggie. She doubted very much they'd be using the Leopold Road exit. Out from under the cover of trees, it was slightly lighter here, the streetlamps from Leopold giving the sky a greyish hue. The three silhouettes ahead went to the second exit along, which came out in a work yard with multiple Portakabins in a row. A lamppost shone in the corner, lighting a part of the area but keeping the rest in darkness.

Roach tugged his captive towards the light, Boycie following and Precious bringing up the rear. Roach had already scouted this place for cameras in case Precious or Boycie had to run from their selling spots to hide. Thankfully, there weren't any. Then she laughed at her thoughts—because he'd be fucking stupid to bring someone here if there were.

For the first time, she got a look at the person whose arm Roach gripped. He must have cable tied his wrists together behind him, and material filled his mouth. Having sunglasses on meant Precious couldn't see him as clearly as she wanted, but her view was good enough to know he was shitting himself.

"Now then," Roach said. "My mate here told you if you fuck us about and don't pay what you owe in time, then you're going to meet your maker. I reckon you

thought he was joking. You thought because we're young, we couldn't pull it off. Have you not heard about me murdering people before? Didn't you believe the stories? My other friend here, she's going to be the one to slit your throat. She's already got a knife in her hand, look. She's nothing but diligent."

A dark puddle crept from beneath the man's feet where he'd pissed himself. His grey tracksuit bottoms showed evidence of urine stains. He was a skinny type with a rat face that belonged on a lot of heroin addicts. The sunken eyes and the loss of teeth showed exactly what he got up to.

"I'm sorry," he whimpered around the material, or at least it sounded like that.

Precious examined her emotions and wasn't surprised to find she didn't care what this bloke's excuses were. She didn't care if he had kids—who were better off without him anyway—and she didn't care if he had a woman at home. He was a waster, that much was obvious, hooked and unlikely to get himself off the gear. He probably didn't even want to, he was too far gone.

Her back to the Portakabins, and even though their faces were covered, she had a moment of panic. What if the cabins had cameras inside them? What if they recorded them right now?

She passed that information to Roach. "So we should go. At least to the alley, then we can leave his body in the park."

He didn't answer but tugged Ratty along, Boycie on his other side. They marched him through the exit and into the darkness of the park. Precious was going to have to do this by feel alone; she had no chance of properly seeing what she was doing.

A light flashed on, illuminating Ratty and Roach — Boycie with a torch. Precious darted her gaze around to check where the houses were and whether anyone would see what was happening from that far away, but thankfully, they stood in a little recessed area. She stepped in front of Ratty. What did he see with the light coming from behind her? Did she present as just a creepy silhouette?

Roach held Ratty's upper arms and leaned back a bit, probably so she didn't nick him with the blade by accident. She took another step forward and rested the edge of the knife at the side of Ratty's neck. She had no feelings whatsoever except to get the job done and earn herself three grand. She swiped from left to right, cocking her head to watch the blood sheeting out of the wide slit she'd created. Roach held him up for a moment or two, then he hauled him into the darkness.

Boycie aimed the torch beam at the grass and the blood on it, probably so Precious and Roach didn't step in it. The last thing they needed was to take it home with them, although would any splashes have got on her jacket when she'd made the slice?

"Come on, we need to go and burn our clothes." Roach walked out of the darkness and into the light. "You did good, Presh."

"I want that three grand in my hand by the morning."

He nodded. "Of course, what do you fucking take me for?"

"Just reminding you my services don't come for free." She wanted to say he'd have to pay her for sex if he wanted it, too, but she held off in front of Boycie.

The light doused, and at first, she wasn't sure which direction he headed off in, but Boycie must have reached a hand out, because fingers curled around hers, and she stumbled along towards the green on Reginald. Roach had probably parked his car somewhere there.

She examined her feelings again.
Nothing.
Sweet fuck all.
Good.

Chapter Nineteen

Boycie had sat in his car around the side of the Orange Lantern all night. He'd browsed his phone to pass the time, glancing up every so often when he caught sight of the shadow of someone either approaching the house or leaving it. He hadn't told Precious he was there; he didn't want to give her the chance to go to Edna's via the back way. And he reckoned she would. She'd already gone against their plan with Kayla, and he doubted anything would stop her from doing it again—unless he was there to physically do it.

Ever since he'd thought about her killing Cooper, too, he couldn't get it out of his head. That was her bloody plan, wasn't it? It had to be. And he'd give it to her, they'd both been stupid to only think of killing the two women. Cooper had also been involved, playing the part of Vicky's boyfriend, a bloke called Parker, so he knew what had gone on, too. While Boycie didn't think Cooper was the type to open his gob and blab, Precious might still want to make him disappear.

Silly scenarios kept popping into Boycie's head. What if Precious had stolen Kayla's flat keys after she'd sliced her throat? What if she let herself in and killed Cooper in his bed while he slept? It was the type of thing she'd do as well. She could even go back to Skein Road to murder him on another night, but Boycie would have to warn her against that regardless of whether it pissed her off, because even though the neighbours down there weren't the best at reporting things to the police, hence Cooper dealing there in the first place, they'd probably be on the lookout now for Kayla's killer coming back. There was more chance that Precious would get caught.

For the umpteenth time tonight, Boycie contemplated ringing The Brothers and telling them everything, then he pushed that thought away. He couldn't stand to watch Precious strung up in that weird metal room and killed in front of him. And honestly, she didn't deserve that—the torture was insane. He laughed at how weird that sounded. How could she *not* deserve to die after what she'd done? The same went for him. He'd done some wicked things while working for Roach. He supposed he was against Precious and her antics now because since Roach had died, he'd wanted to lead a better life. Going to the twins about Roach had made him see that it wasn't so bad trying to be a better person after all. He'd become tired of being a thug, Roach's right-hand man, the one who beat people up to send a message. Now he didn't have to do it, he was more at peace—except Precious was ruining that.

Maybe he ought to move away, leave her to it. Distance himself from this whole bloody estate, start again elsewhere. When the flats and Roach's house were signed over to him, he could sell them and piss off abroad without looking back. The only problem with that was Precious would have nowhere to live, and she might turn on Boycie and tell the twins he was in on Alice's murder.

He played a few levels of *Piggy Kingdom*, passing another hour. Then he got out of the car and stood by the corner of the house so he could see Precious leaving. He only had to wait ten minutes and she stepped outside, dressed all in black. It was obvious she planned to still go to Edna's. Were those the clothes she'd worn to kill Kayla?

"I'll give you a lift home."

She jumped and whipped her head round to stare at him in the shadows. The orange bulb in the light beside the front door gave her a peach glow, and for a moment she seemed frozen in time.

"What the fuck are you doing here?" she whispered, a scowl forming.

"Like I said, I'll give you a lift home."

"I'm not going home and you know it."

"I think you ought to, don't you? Doing them both within a matter of hours isn't a good idea, Presh."

"What are you talking about?"

"Don't play dumb. Cooper phoned me. You slashed Kayla's throat on Skein Road."

Her shoulders sagged—did she think Cooper had seen her do it? "Who else did he phone?"

"The Brothers. The police."

"Does anyone suspect me?"

"Why would they?"

"I don't know, I just…"

"Were you *actually* going to go to Edna's in a minute? Really?"

She shrugged again. "I don't like the sound of where this conversation's going. If I want to go there, that's my business. I don't have to answer to you."

"You do if you expect me to be your alibi. Can you at least wait a month until the Kayla thing dies down?"

"Look, only we know Edna and Kayla are linked in some way. Oh, and Cooper knows, but can you see him going to The Brothers or the police about it when he played his part as Parker?"

"I can actually." That was a lie. *Will she take the bait, prove my suspicions?*

"Then we should bump him off, too. I don't know why we didn't think of it in the first place."

There we go. This chat had gone exactly the way he'd wanted it to. "Then we need to plan this properly. I mean it, it's too serious to just jump in half-cocked."

She walked towards him, which was a good sign. It meant she might get in the car. "But you agree he has to go, yes? We need to get rid of *all* loose ends."

Boycie hated to admit it, but the only loose end he was worried about was Precious. *Loose cannon, more like.* He'd loved her since they were children. They'd been best friends for years. But he couldn't risk her blabbing about his involvement in certain things. And she would. She'd go down fighting, taking him with her. The horrible thought that he'd have to get rid of her himself sent his skin cold.

Jesus Christ, there must be another way.

But there wasn't. She was too headstrong. She'd never back down. Even if Boycie fucked off and got away from her, there was still a risk she'd drop him in it later down the line, and he wasn't prepared to risk that. He was as selfish as her and as selfish as Roach. All three of them had always been out for themselves. They'd pretended they were a secure trio and always had each other's backs, but individually, they'd only had themselves in mind.

Part of him felt sad that he'd never have the kind of relationship he'd always wanted with Precious. Settling down, getting married, having kids, but there were more important things he had to do in order to remain safe. He quickly formed a plan, right up until after she'd died. Yeah, he could come out of this looking innocent—so long as Cooper played ball.

"Right," he said, "listen to me. I'm not trying to tell you what to do, but seriously, the police are crawling all over Skein Road, so you need to be careful now. Leave Edna, *please*. We have to create a solid plan and look at all eventualities so there's no way we're going to get caught."

"But what if Edna hears about Kayla—which she will—and she decides it's too much to handle and opens her mouth?"

He'd have to pacify her. "Okay, I get what you're saying. We'll sit up all night if we have to and talk it through."

She seemed to believe him, because she nodded and stalked past him round the corner to the car. He hurried after her in case she legged it through the back garden, but she stood by the passenger door. She got in and put her seat belt on.

He stared at her for a moment, remembering all the things they done together, all the laughs they'd had, all the promises they'd made. His eyes stung. Was he really going to do this? Get rid of his best friend—again?

Is there any other choice?

No, Precious was too stubborn to back down, and she was going to end up putting him right in the shit. He loved her, that wasn't in dispute, but he'd still kill her.

Self-preservation at its finest.

He didn't believe Cooper needed to die, and anyway, he was too scared of Boycie to open his mouth to the twins. So long as Boycie was in the clear, he didn't give a shit *what* he had to do to achieve it. It was going to hurt, murdering one of his friends, someone who'd turned into his lover and the person he thought he'd have stayed with for the rest of his life, but shit happened, and he just had to deal with it.

He got in the car. On the drive, as he'd predicted and true to form, she remained stubbornly silent. It would be to either punish him for ordering her about again, which was how she'd see it, or she was pissed off she'd been stopped from killing Edna. She was likely thinking that once he'd dropped her at her flat, they had a chat, and then he went home, she could go back out again and walk to the bungalow. She was probably thinking a million things, except for the fact that the man sitting beside her was planning to kill her.

She'd laugh in anyone's face if they told her that's what he had in mind—this time yesterday, *he'd* have laughed. She thought he'd do anything for her, and while he'd made it look like he would, he'd kept a part of himself back. He knew her of old. He knew how quickly she could turn on someone when they didn't do what she wanted or she couldn't get her own way. If she had to, she'd ditch him in a heartbeat, and he had a feeling she was heading that way—knowing her, she'd cause little arguments so he got naffed off and ended the relationship.

He wasn't stupid, he knew he wasn't the man for her. He had hoped he was at the start, but having spent a lot of time with her lately, he'd realised she'd used him in order to tell The

Brothers about Roach so they killed him. She didn't really want to be with Boycie.

It was a bitter pill to swallow, but there was time enough to cry about it later.

He took a turning that led to the road that went past Daffodil Woods. It was the safest place to do it. They'd come here a few times in the past with Roach to sit and talk through their plans. All right, those times they'd brought a blanket and a picnic, but maybe she wouldn't think it was odd that he'd brought her here now.

She laughed. "God, we haven't come here to make plans for ages."

"I thought it'd make us take this more seriously."

"Me, you mean."

"Yeah. You've got to admit you've been a pain in the arse about these murders. You've always been impatient." He parked in a clearing and switched the engine off. With no headlights on, they sat in complete darkness. "I've always loved you, you know that, right?"

"Yes…"

"And if there was any other way, I'd take it."

"What are you talking about?"

"I'm sorry things couldn't work out between us. I'm sorry you used me. I'm sorry I realised that. Sorry about a lot of things."

"Have you been drinking or something?"

"No, I'm stone-cold sober, which is why this hurts even more."

"What hurts?"

She had no clue, did she. No bloody idea about what was going through his mind. Did it mean she trusted him not to put his hands around her throat and squeeze? To pull his knife out of his pocket and slice her throat like she'd sliced Kayla's? Did she believe she was so safe with him she didn't need to worry? It was sad, really, when he thought about it that way; he was about to murder someone who trusted him.

Don't think about that. She'd throw you to the wolves if it meant saving herself.

He unclipped his seat belt and straddled her. She didn't seem tense. Her breathing hadn't sped up. She must think he wanted sex. There was something awful about knowing you were going to throttle someone when it was the last thing they thought you'd do. It felt wrong, but he'd made his mind up. He slotted his hands around her throat and positioned his thumbs over her Adam's apple.

Her laugh came out unsteady. "I didn't realise you were into that sort of shit. Kinky sod."

"There are a lot of things you don't know about me." *And you'll have no time to figure out what they are.* "Did you think I didn't know what you were up to?"

"What are you on about?"

"I think you thought at the beginning that you could make a go of it with me, then you realised you couldn't. But instead of finishing it, you chose to carry on. To use me. But then, you've been using me all along, haven't you? You needed me to go with you to the twins, to grass Roach up—with two of us doing it, it looked more convincing. We promised we'd be a team and we'd always tell each other everything, but you never told me you were going to do Kayla so soon. There's probably loads of shit you've lied to me about. Stuff you've hidden."

He squeezed harder.

"Pack it in," Precious said, her voice croaky.

"I can't."

What did he mean? What was he saying, that he was going to *kill* her? She quickly thought back over what he'd just said, and fuck, he knew what she'd done and why. He knew damn well she'd used him. And there she'd been, thinking she was so clever, fooling him. That had been Kayla's problem, too. The pair of them had thought they could act like bitches and keep getting away with it.

"Please," she begged, hating that she sounded so weak, her voice barely there. "We can fix this. You don't have to do this."

"That's where you're wrong. I don't trust you anymore, and when the trust is gone, then everything goes to shit. I fucking loved you so much."

"You still can…" God, her throat hurt. "I…" She couldn't force any more words out, he was squeezing too hard. She felt herself drifting, her consciousness going.

She didn't expect to think of her parents come the end, but they popped into her head all the same. Mum always worrying about the trouble her daughter would bring to her door, Dad encouraging it. That first walk to school… Now

Precious could see it through an adult's eyes, Mum had been crying as she'd turned at the gate. She'd been upset that her little girl was growing up. Or maybe she'd cried with guilt because she'd felt so bloody relieved to get shot of her during the day.

Mum must have lived on her nerves half the time.

Precious drifted some more, wishing she'd done a few things differently when it came to how she'd treated her poor mother, but for the most part, she had no regrets. Apart from Boycie knowing what she was up to all along and she hadn't suspected a thing.

Blackness called to her, but she fought it. Got a second wind from somewhere. Fuck was she dying like this.

Boycie's eyes burned again, so he closed them and did what he had to do. She struggled beneath him, her hands coming up to try to prise his wrists away from her to relieve the pressure. She must have known he was too strong for her, yet in good old Precious fashion, she carried on anyway, yet a few seconds ago, he'd thought she'd given up. She drummed her feet in the footwell, and he imagined it was around about now that she was panicking—proper panicking; she knew this was the end, and she probably couldn't believe it was him doing the killing. She'd have thought he'd have walked to the ends of the earth for her, and at one time, he would, but once he'd suspected she was using him, he'd hardened his heart towards her.

"Neither of us were honest with each other," he said. "I'll see you on the other side."

She renewed her efforts to get him off her. He gritted his teeth and carried on, giving one good push with his thumbs. Something in her neck broke; he felt it give. Hot tears burned his cheeks, and a lump expanded in his throat. He hated himself for this, for hoping that when he contacted The Brothers they'd make her body disappear as if she'd just gone missing. No closure for her parents.

His arms ached, but he continued on way past the time she'd gone limp. Eventually, he released the pressure and got off her, getting out of the car and slamming the door. Sucking in the cold air, he bent over, hands on his knees, and sobbed for the loss of someone he'd thought was his best friend. He let it all out for God knew how long, then straightened, resolved to get this next part over and done with.

He took his phone out of his pocket and dialled Cooper. "Listen to me, this is serious. Precious admitted to me that she killed Kayla. I just fucking strangled her, I was so fucking angry, and she's dead."

"What the fuck?"

"I know, but get this. She said about going after Edna an' all, and you. For all I fucking know, she could have been planning to kill me, too. All because of Alice. So this is why I need you to listen. I've got a dead body in my car and no way to get rid of it, so I'm going to have to ask the twins for help. When they come to speak to you, which they will, you have to make out you have no idea what they're talking about with regards to Kayla being Vicky. If they bring up your alias of Parker, you claim you don't know what they mean. We *have* to keep ourselves out of this shit. If they find out we knew about the Alice murder plot, we're fucked, mate. I get that this is a lot on top of Kayla dying, but we have to save ourselves and grieve later."

"I just... I mean, what the pissing hell?"

"I know. Precious went off the rails. She was convinced everyone would grass her up for killing Alice, so she had to get rid of everybody. She sounded completely unhinged, off her fucking rocker. I didn't want to have to kill her, but it was the only way we could stay safe. Remember what I said? You don't know who Parker is. You don't know who Vicky is. You didn't know Kayla was Vicky. You got that?"

"Yes."

"Right, I need to let The Brothers know. And I'm sorry about Kayla. I had no idea what Precious was up to."

Boycie rang the twins. It took a while for them to answer.

"We're a bit busy at the minute," George said. "I suppose I did tell you to ring me if there were any more developments, but..."

"It was Precious."

"It was Precious what?"

"She killed Kayla."

"You what?"

"I picked her up from work at the Lantern, and on the way home she told me what she'd done — for Roach. She killed Alice. *She* was the fucking biker. Kayla was someone called Vicky, and Precious worried she was going to crack and admit her part in it. I had no clue about any of this. I fucking lost it and killed her."

"What?"

"I strangled her and I'm in Daffodil Woods and I don't know what to do."

"Jesus Christ. Okay, stay where you are and someone will come and help you. He's Irish, and that's all you need to know."

"What will he do?"

"Take Precious, then you'll go home and forget all about this."

"How can I forget? I thought she was my best mate. She kept shit from me. She was in on everything with that fucking Roach. The pair of them are arseholes."

"Betrayal is a bit of a wanker, but you'll have to get over it. What about Kayla's bloke? Do you think he knew?"

"Cooper? Fuck, no. I just rang him to ask him, and he had no idea what I was talking about. I warned him I was telling you about Kayla and you might go round to speak to him, and he didn't seem like he was worried. Sounds like the pair of us had the wool pulled over our eyes by women."

"Sorry to sound like I don't give a shit, but we're up to our armpits here with something else, and the last thing we needed was another body on our hands. I get why you killed her. I'm glad you did it, because it saved me a job, but what's done is done. Sit tight. Our man won't be long."

The line went dead, and he leaned his backside against the car. He phoned Cooper again so they could get their stories straighter. He reiterated how important it was to not fuck this up.

"I'm going to have to kill Edna after this Irish bloke's picked Precious up. I didn't want to have to do it, but now's the perfect chance because if they make the link, Precious will get the blame. Fuck's sake."

"What a bloody shit show. Do you need any help?" Cooper asked.

"No, it's best you stay out of it. For all we know the police could be watching you because of Kayla."

"One of them told me they think she was killed by either a druggie or someone against druggies. I don't think they're looking at me for it."

"It doesn't matter. Stay under the radar when it comes to selling drugs, too. Be extra careful. The twins are likely to come round and ask you questions. Just do what I said and act how I told you and everything will be all right."

He could only hope that was true.

Chapter Twenty

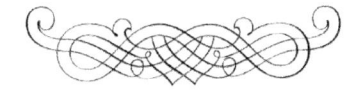

Ichabod always enjoyed these little forays into the dark side. He loved his job at Jackpot Palace but missed being out and about in the thick of things. He'd thought his extra work was over for the night, but he'd been summoned to help the twins out again. As he drove up the track of Daffodil Woods in another stolen car with fake plates, a balaclava covering his features and night-vision goggles over his eyes, he contemplated what he'd find. George had mentioned a man with a body that needed collecting but not much else. His headlights picked out the shape of a car in the distance and a man standing beside it. Ichabod rolled closer, and the man grew agitated, a frown firmly in place.

"What the feckin' hell's this eejit gone and done tae get himself so wound up?"

Killing someone is more than enough, remember.

Hmm, sometimes he forgot that part.

He studied the fella again. It was obvious he wasn't comfortable in this situation. Was this his first kill? Or if it wasn't, was he anxious about who he was about to meet? If Ichabod put himself in his shoes, he supposed it *would* be daunting to wait for a stranger to come and clean up your mess. You had no clue if you could trust them, plus, Ichabod had seen the man's face, but the man couldn't see his.

If he didn't kill someone in the first place, he wouldn't be *in a mess.*

He shouldn't be so judgmental. He'd fucked up in the past. Everyone was entitled to make mistakes.

He parked up, shut the engine off, and got out of the car. In full forensic gear, he walked round to open the boot, then went towards the man who stared at him, wide-eyed, his features green-tinged through the goggle lenses.

Ichabod held up his gloved hands. "I know, I look like someone out of a feckin' alien film. What's ye name?"

"Boycie."

"All right. That what ye mammy called ye, is it, or do ye have another, proper name?"

"I've got a proper one but don't use it."

Ichabod shrugged. "I suppose I don't need tae know what it is. If the twins think ye're all right, then I'll be all right wid ye. Let's have a look at the body then."

Boycie pointed towards the other side of his car. Ichabod took it that he didn't want to go over and see the results of his handiwork. Guilt? Probably. Ichabod rounded the vehicle, expecting to find the deceased on the ground, but no one was there. He peered through the passenger window. A woman, thickened tongue protruding like the head of a purple snake.

"Lover's tiff?" he asked.

"No. She told me she'd killed someone. I lost the plot."

"It happens."

Ichabod returned to his boot and took a black bag off a new roll. Back at the other car, he opened the door and reached over to unclip her seat belt. Drew the bag over her head to contain her hair, tying it in a knot at her bruised neck.

So fella-me-lad strangled her, then.

He hefted her out, dragging her towards his car. Her trainers bumped over the ground, her hands trailing in the fallen leaves, creating a woodland symphony of crackles and shushes. He lifted her into the boot and placed her on her side, tucking her knees up, folding her arms around them. With the bag covering her features, she was now just a nameless item, something to be transported and disposed of.

"Has she got family who'll ask questions?" he called out.

The man came closer. "Yeah, her mum and dad."

"Will it be ye they ask?"

"I expect so."

"I don't envy ye then." Ichabod slammed the boot shut.

He got in the car and drove out of the woods, heading for the cottage. He parked out the front and knocked on the door. George answered, and at the flick of Ichabod's head, he followed him to the boot. Together they carried her inside the cottage, into the steel room where Greg leaned against the wall, maybe having a breather. He held a mop, a bucket nearby. The woman from earlier no longer hung from the ceiling, the trapdoor closed. They must have hidden her beneath the cottage. George guided them over to the corner, and they propped the new woman up against the wall.

"We've had a bit of a night," Ichabod said.

"You could say that." George smiled. "Still, it's almost over. But we're going to run out of space under this fucking cottage before long. I'd have got you to take her to the warehouse, but with the CCTV keep being switched off, it'll create suspicion. We'll have to find a new location by the river so we can dump the chopped-up body parts in there."

"Will ye sell the warehouse?"

"Not with all that DNA in there, no. Bleach can mask it, but it's all still there. We'll take the rack down and bring it here, plus all the medieval tools and shit. Then there's the clean tracksuits and whatnot. Fucking hell, we haven't really got the room for it in here."

"We'll put in one of the bedrooms," Greg said. "It's not like anyone stays here, is it, so it won't be in the way."

Ichabod sighed, tired to his bones. "Is that me done, then?"

George nodded. "Cheers for your help, mate."

"Who was she?" Ichabod jerked his thumb towards the woman with the bag on her head.

"Someone who made us believe she was telling us the truth when it came to that Roach stuff. Turns out, she wasn't—she'd kept a bit of info back. Her being murdered, it saved us a job."

"Anythin' else ye need me tae do before I go back tae the casino?"

"Nah, just dump the car and let Dwayne know where to pick it up."

Ichabod said his goodbyes and left the cottage. He'd burn his outfit round the back of Jackpot Palace later in a drum and flush the ashes down the toilet. He took the route that led him past

Daffodil Woods and couldn't help but go up the track again to check if that bloke had gone. Some people couldn't get past the fact they'd killed, and Ichabod worried the daft prick had sat on the ground and cried. Lost the plot even more. But he wasn't there, so he continued on his own journey, working out where to leave the car for Dwayne where there were no cameras and it wasn't that far for him to walk back to Jackpot Palace.

There were still a couple of hours of gambling left in the night yet.

Chapter Twenty-One

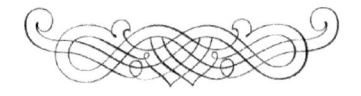

Edna lay on her bed in the dark, staring at the ceiling. She'd been scatterbrained and had yet to set up her cameras which had arrived late in the evening, so she hadn't been able to sleep for worrying about the peeper coming back. She'd do it in the morning, although it was technically morning now. Five o'clock wasn't any time to be getting up; she'd hated having to do that when she'd worked for the twins at Haven. She'd needed to be at the refuge in time to cook breakfast. Now she wasn't there anymore, she enjoyed her lie-ins.

Would she be safe to close her eyes now? Surely no one would come to kill her this early. Whoever it was who stared at her through the window might not want to risk being seen now. It would be all right to shut her eyes, wouldn't it?

She allowed them to drift closed. They stung from being so gritty. She rubbed at them, knuckling so hard that white spots danced. She rolled onto her side, facing away from the window, too tired to even bother shutting the curtains. It was still dark outside anyway.

That sinking sensation into the mattress pulled her towards dreamland.

She jolted upright at the sound of her patio door being slid across. Shit, she'd forgotten to check it was locked. Had she even fallen asleep? Heart rate escalating, she checked the window. Still dark. She got out of bed and snatched up the knife she'd taken to keeping on the nightstand. She moved to lean against the wall beside her door which stood open a tad, giving her a view through the living room doorway. Although it was dark, she still made out a shadow shape that shouldn't be there. A person.

"Who's there?" she called, then felt stupid because whoever it was wasn't exactly going to introduce themselves, were they. "I'm phoning the police, so you'd better fuck off, *now*."

They ignored her and came to the living room doorway. They stood inside the frame, arms bowed, legs planted a foot apart.

"Edna?" they whispered.

"*Boycie*?" she said. "What are *you* doing here? We agreed we wouldn't speak to each other after my job was over at Haven. And how did you open that patio door? I swore I locked it last night."

"I used a pick, and the reason I'm here is because something bad has happened."

"What is it?"

Boycie stepped further into the hallway. "Kayla's dead."

"Oh shit! How come?"

"The person who killed Alice was worried about Kayla opening her mouth. What if they come for you next? I came here to warn you to be careful."

It made sense now. "Someone's been watching me for ages. They stand in my back garden and stare at me through the bedroom window in the middle of the night. I bought cameras to catch them at it but haven't got round to setting them up yet."

"I'll sort that for you later. We'll have a cup of tea first. You go and get showered and dressed. I'll stick the kettle on."

Relieved it was only Boycie and not some creepy bastard she had to fight off, Edna did as she was told. She hoped he wasn't going to stay too long. She had to go and do some baking at the Noodle and wanted him out of her way before then.

Under the spray of water, she planned which recipes she was going to try. Lemon drizzle cake and chocolate brownies to start. If Nessa liked those and agreed they could be sold, then Edna's new life could begin.

Gloves on, Boycie found Edna's bi-polar tablets in one of the kitchen cupboards. Thankfully, they were the plastic capsule type, where he could pull the two sides apart and put the powder into a cup. He used the whole packet, then did the same again with a few boxes of paracetamol he'd brought with him, shoving the empty boxes in his pocket afterwards.

He had no clue what lithium tasted like, so maybe she'd know there was something off with her tea, but he hoped the whiskey in a hip flask he'd popped into his pocket before coming here would disguise any taste. She'd likely ask why he'd put alcohol in her drink, so he'd have to make out he never drank his without it.

Whatever. If she gave him any gyp, he'd shove a sock in her gob and tie her up until the tea went cold and then he'd force her to drink it. He'd bought a small funnel and a short length of hose with him so he could shove it down her throat if need be. He wasn't pissing about here. This was serious, and she had to die. Yes, there'd be a post-mortem because it was a suicide and they'd likely detect whether something had been pushed down her throat, but this had to be done. Sadly, he didn't think Edna would purposely tell anybody about the Alice murder plot, but he just couldn't leave it to chance.

She appeared in the kitchen, chattering about a job opportunity at the Noodle. His guts rolled over. The thought of her working for the twins and accidentally blurting something out left him cold. Yeah, this was the right decision, and unfortunately, if Cooper seemed like he was going to be a problem in the future, he'd have to go, too. Boycie hated the fact that Precious was right, and that he could have been right, too, in that she'd planned to kill them all.

He handed Edna her tea as she sat at the table covered in all manner of shit. "That's got a bit of booze in it. Sorry, it's a habit of mine. I didn't think to ask whether you'd prefer it without."

"It's all right, I could do with a bit of Dutch courage. I'm nervous about going to the Noodle, even though I know I can bake really well. Knowing my luck, the cakes will get burnt today."

Guilt poked him really hard. At long last, Edna had found the right path, and he was about to take it away from her. If he was any kind of decent bloke, he'd kill himself instead and leave Edna and Cooper to get on with their lives. But he wasn't decent, he was a bastard. Okay, he had a heart, but it wasn't big enough to allow her to continue breathing.

She sipped away at the tea, guffing on about lemon drizzle cakes and chocolate brownies, maybe some shortbread biscuits if she had time. "I've got to get to the supermarket an' all because I doubt Nessa will have all the ingredients I need."

You won't make it to the supermarket, love.

He could see it in his head. Edna all but skipping to Tesco, her hopes and dreams brimming inside her. A part of him wanted her to experience that, and he fought the urge to get up and walk out. He let her prattle on, seeing her 'vision for the future' as she described it.

"But don't you think the twins will find it a bit odd?" he said.

"What do you mean?"

"You're called Edna. The woman at Haven was called Edna. Both of you are good at baking. They're going to put two and two together, aren't they?"

She frowned. "I don't feel very well."

"Christ, it's probably the whiskey too early in the morning. Come on, I'll help you back to bed."

"But I need to be at the pub by ten."

"It's okay, I'll make sure to wake you up in time."

She allowed him to hold her, and he led her across the hallway to her room. She flopped onto the mattress, her skin a strange pale shade. A sheen of sweat covered her face, and he reckoned she was going to puke. He needed those drugs to stay inside her and panicked in case she vomited.

She groaned and moved onto her side, her back to the window, and within seconds, her breathing went heavy and her eyes closed. A soft snore escaped. He stood in her room for a long time. Could have been an hour, could have been two, until her chest stopped moving.

He left the bungalow and closed the patio door so the lock clicked. Edna was a loner, so none of her neighbours would take any notice that she hadn't shown her face for a few days. Although now Nessa was expecting her to turn up to do some baking, that might pose a problem. But would she bother to follow up why Edna hadn't turned up? She'd likely just shrug it off because Edna was a known druggie and unreliable.

He couldn't think about that now. He adjusted his mouth mask and walked along the street, hunching his shoulders and keeping his face down. He wouldn't draw attention, loads of people still wore Covid masks these days. He dipped down streets and rounded corners, taking a convoluted route so he didn't create a direct path to home. He entered his place, relieved to be back, then phoned Cooper.

"Any news for me?" Boycie asked.

"No, nothing. What about you?"

"Edna's been dealt with. The twins sent someone to take Precious' body away. We're in the clear."

"Right. So what do I do now that Skein Road is out of the equation regarding selling drugs?"

"It's your job and your decision, but maybe just use the other location for now. There's going to be too much heat for you to continue at Skein. Just watch your back because the police might be surveilling you. They might have said they don't think you had anything to do with Kayla, but what they say and what they think are two different things. Never trust a copper."

He ended the call and went for a shower. Climbed into bed, desperate for sleep. Tears fell. He was never going to see Precious again, and it hurt. Why did she have to be such a stubborn bitch? Why couldn't she have just listened to him?

He drifted off with no answers to those questions.

Chapter Twenty-Two

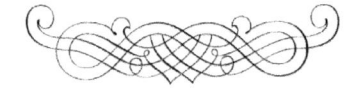

Precious had been instrumental in helping Roach set up the Orange Lantern. She'd had a vision in mind of how it would work, and he'd actually gone with her recommendations. On one hand, it pleased her when he did that, but on the other, it naffed her off, especially because he was going around saying it had all been his idea. Boycie knew the truth, so that was

something, but the sex workers at the Lantern thought Roach was amazing. Precious wanted them protected, not to be used and abused. She wanted them to work there knowing they were safe and looked after. The workers gushed at him, though, thinking he'd been the mastermind behind their well-being. Precious had said she'd run the place, but he'd overridden that and brought someone called Widow in.

That had naffed her off, too, although she'd soon got used to it. And considering how much work Widow had to do prior to opening night, Precious was kind of glad she'd been demoted—that's how she saw it anyway, because in her head, the main job had been hers all along. All she had to do now was flirt and swan around the living room making sure the men were happy. The only other job Roach allowed her to do was interview any sex workers and give them positions if she felt they'd be good at their job. Widow wasn't allowed the last say on that either, so Precious supposed she should be chuffed that Roach trusted her that much.

The Orange Lantern was opening tonight, and Precious stood in the hallway waiting for the first knock on the door. Word had been bandied around that a new massage parlour with extras had opened, but she worried that the people who'd been told were the skagheads and the skanks who bought gear off Roach's runners. But somehow, he'd spread the news to decent-looking people, because when she opened the front door, two gentlemen stood there in suits.

She greeted them with a smile. "Good evening. If you can have your identification ready, please…"

One of them stared at her funny. "I can't be having my wife finding out about this."

"Don't worry, it's just for me to see something official to know you're not a weirdo."

She'd already said to Roach that men could have fake credentials, but he'd wanted to maintain the upper hand by asking for ID. He reckoned it would make the place look more upmarket.

"I literally just need a quick glance," she said.

Both of them produced drivers licences, held them up quickly, then stuffed them back in their wallets. She couldn't blame them for the speed, they wouldn't want their names memorised. Still, she'd done what Roach had requested and then let them in, taking them to the living room.

"Here are the brochures. They contain pictures and descriptions of each lady who specialises in massage. We cater to sports injuries, back strains, sore necks, tense shoulders, you get the gist."

They nodded. The one with the wife chose a blonde, and the other opted for a brunette. She took a deep breath and launched herself into the next part of her job. She felt stupid at first, flirting, but once they laughed at her jokes, she relaxed and settled into her role.

Two more men arrived, and she went through the same spiel. A soft-sounding buzzer alerted her that the women upstairs were now ready. One of the new men had also chosen the same brunette, so she told him he'd either have to wait or he'd have to pick another. He opted to wait.

"If you'll excuse me for a moment." She left the living room to walk down the hallway to Widow's office where a young woman waited to escort the men upstairs. She tapped on the door and poked her head around. "They all seem legit," she whispered, "so they can be shown upstairs now."

Widow nodded and gestured to her computer screen. "I've been watching them, and I agree. None of them seem suspicious. Off you go, Amanda. If any of them are inappropriate, you let me know."

Amanda scuttled out, and Precious followed her so she could continue flirting with the man who'd stayed behind. He seemed too young to be here, too good-looking, and she was tempted to ask him what his story was. However, Roach had said these men wouldn't want anyone knowing their business, and their visits to a brothel were likely kept a secret.

Err, since when did you do as you were told?

"Do you have a girlfriend?" Naughty of her, and he might not even answer truthfully, but she wasn't in the mood to pretend she fancied him and to giggle like a schoolgirl.

"No, I don't have the time for a proper relationship."

"Had enough of you right hand, have you?" She laughed to take the sting of what had come out as an accusation when she hadn't meant it to be.

"Something like that. To be honest, I've got no confidence when it comes to women, so it's easier if I just come to places like this."

"Why would you need confidence to see a massage therapist?" she asked.

"I've still got to take some of my clothes off, haven't I?"

He'd passed her test with his answer, although he could still be a police officer. Not that she really thought he was, but Roach had warned her to keep her eyes and ears open. She doubted she'd ever fully relax while she worked here, always on the lookout for the plod.

"You don't have to flirt with me," he said on a sigh. "It makes me uncomfortable anyway. I can't even fucking pretend to be good at it myself." He laughed away his embarrassment.

She never really felt sorry for anyone, her empathy level was at zero, but she sort *of had sympathy for him. Fancy being that handsome and having to come here. She'd thought the lush ones had all the confidence in the world, but obviously not.*

"You'll be all right when you meet the right one," she said and sat on the sofa, crossing her legs.

"But how will I meet her? I work all day and I haven't got the guts to go into a pub."

"What about going with your mates?"

He shrugged. "I don't actually have any. Well, not around here anyway. I left them all behind when I moved to London."

Her empathy had dried up now. He was having a pity party, and she wasn't prepared to accept the invite to join in. She now had the feeling he was taking the piss out of her, making out he didn't have any confidence when he likely had it in spades. She supposed she'd meet all different kinds of men here, and she'd learn to know who was lying and who wasn't. Usually she'd call him out and tell him she knew exactly what he was playing at, but as this was her job now, she should actually follow some rules. She'd hate it, but if she wanted to remain here and scoop up the position of manager by getting rid of Widow somehow, then that's what she'd have to do.

"How did it go?" Roach asked at the end of the night, or should that be the early hours of the morning.

It was four a.m., and Precious was knackered from standing on her feet the whole time. She sat on the sofa in the living room, sensing Roach was about to give her the third degree. "If you wanted to know how the night went so much, you should have fucking stayed here." If he didn't trust Widow's interpretation of the past few hours, which she'd given to him before she'd left, then he had a control problem. But he was that much of a gloater, he probably wanted to hear Precious repeat that the first night had been a huge success.

She told him her evening from start to finish, and he was grinning by the end of it. "I'm not working that many hours again, though, not in a row like that. Nine hours on my feet was a fucking nightmare. I suggest I work from ten p.m. until three. We can employ some other women to greet and flirt while I'm not here.

There's bound to be friends of the sex workers who'll be willing to step up."

"It sounds like you're making decisions all by yourself, Presh." Roach narrowed his eyes at her. "And you know how much that dogs me off."

"But I was here all night; I know what's needed, you don't. Ask Widow, she'd say the same thing. She'll also need someone to help her run the place while she's not here, especially if you're on about opening during the day, too. What was it you said, to maximise profits?"

"Just remember your place, that's all," he said.

She was about to blast him a new arsehole, but a tap at the front door had them both stiffening. The customers and workers had left, as had Widow, only Precious and Roach remaining. Maybe a punter had heard about the place, but not the opening and closing times.

"Should I...?" She gestured to the living room door.

"No. Once people find out we open the door even when we're shut, they'll keep on. There's got to be boundaries. And anyway, it's bound to be someone who wants a fuck, and I can't see you opening your legs to them."

"No thanks."

Roach got up and pulled the side of the curtain across so he could look out. "They're fucking off now, and it's a woman."

Precious shot out of her seat. "What? Let me see." She moved to the window and stared outside. "That's Amanda, you div."

"Well, I didn't know, did I?"

"And that makes my point nicely. You're not here to even know she works for you, I am. There are times when I know what's best and you don't." She walked into the hallway and unlocked the door, stepping outside and quickly rushing towards the pavement. She glanced left and right.

Amanda stood beneath a streetlamp.

"Oh no you don't, not out here." Precious approached her. "What are you bloody doing? Roach is inside, and he'll go mental if he thinks you're touting for business outside the house."

"I didn't make enough this evening. I've got a whole month's rent to cover. My ex came home while I was here. Mum was babysitting, and he used his key, went in anyway. He nicked my housekeeping tin. I reckon if I stand here for long enough, one of the punters will come by and pick me up."

Precious glanced at the house to make sure Roach couldn't see them. Thankfully, a bush was in the way.

She looked back at Amanda. "Come in early tomorrow and get a few extra hours. Not all the positions have been filled yet, don't forget. I'll tell Roach what's happened and he can let Widow know. If you do extra hours for a few days, that should cover your rent, shouldn't it?"

Precious' generosity could be mistaken for kindness, but she had her own agenda here. She didn't want Amanda getting caught moonlighting elsewhere. It was one of Roach's rules that the women who worked at the Orange Lantern couldn't have another job on the side. It would look bad on Precious because she was the one who'd employed Amanda. She didn't want to give Roach any reason to accuse her of being crap at her job.

"Okay," Amanda said. "Yes, that should work."

"Go home before Roach sees you, for fuck's sake."

Amanda crossed the street and walked down a little way, then got in her car and drove off. Precious returned to the house.

Roach waited with his hands on his hips. "Well, what was she doing out there?"

"She knew we'd still be here cleaning up. She's desperate for extra hours, so I told her you'd fix it with Widow—seeing as they all think you're the Messiah. She needs to double what she's down for this week."

"And we can afford for her to stay in her room all day and most of the evening? There are no other women who need her room?"

"We're not at full staff capacity yet. I told you that this morning."

"Sorry, must have been distracted."

He really did piss her off, but what had she expected? He'd always been the same, ever since she'd first met him.

"Right, I'll message her and let her know you said yes then, shall I?"

"Yeah."

"And what about Widow? Shall I do that or will you?"

He sat on the sofa. "You do it. That's a secretary's job."

She wanted to punch him in the face but got her phone out to get on with it. She had a feeling it was going to be a long old road, fighting him all the way, but eventually she'd make him see she was the best one to run the whole place, and he'd give her Widow's job. All she had to do was prove herself in the meantime.

Chapter Twenty-Three

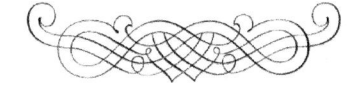

The twins sat in the Noodle, waiting for Edna to turn up. It was past when she was due, so that didn't bode well. George was getting arsier by the minute.

"Where the fuck is she?" he muttered. "I mean, it sounded to me like she wanted to set up her own business, but if she can't even get here at the specified time, it's not like Nessa's going to trust her in future, is it?"

"Maybe she got held up," Greg said.

George threw him a filthy look. "D'you think?"

Greg turned to stare at him. "Don't get funny with me, dickhead. Anyway, something wasn't right yesterday when we learned both the Ednas are bakers, and we should have done something about it then. Come on, we'll go around to her place now."

"But she's only five minutes late."

"Yet you've been moaning about it, so get your arse up and get in that taxi."

They left the Noodle via the back, and Greg drove them to Edna's bungalow, parking out the front. They walked up her garden path, the flower beds as neat as ever. George nosed through a window at a kitchen and craned his neck to try and see through another doorway down the opposite wall a bit. He spotted the end of a bed and the telltale lump of someone's feet beneath a quilt.

"She's fucking overslept," he said.

"Then we'll knock on the door until she wakes up."

Greg hammered on it a few times, but the feet didn't move. Edna must be dead to the world. Now George's dander was up at how cheeky she'd been to ask for a chance at a job and then not even wake up in time to go. He marched round the side of the bungalow to the back and tried the handle of the patio doors, but it didn't budge. He moved along to peer into the next window. A bedroom with a single bed beneath it, Edna fast asleep. It really pissed him off, her lack of regard for Nessa's time. He rapped on the window, the sound deadened by his leather gloves.

"Oi, Edna," he called.

She didn't stir. He looked closer, and now he had, he spotted the skin around her lips had a blue tint. He stared at her arm to see if it went up and down with the rise and fall of her chest, but there was no movement.

"Fuck it."

Thankful they'd decided to wear beards and wigs today, George stormed to the front of the house and curled his finger to beckon Greg over to him. His brother followed him round the back, and George pointed at the window.

Greg stared through it. "Oh, fuck me sideways." He stepped back and glanced at George. "Something shifty is going on. First Kayla and now Edna."

"So what, do we believe Roach planned to kill Kayla and Edna, and Precious fulfilled that, even after he was dead?" George asked.

"Why do you look like you don't believe that when it's plain as day? She admitted to Boycie that she'd killed Alice and Kayla. Kayla and Edna must have known about Alice for Precious to need to shut them up. That was probably the plan all along, to get rid of everyone involved. Who knows, maybe Boycie was next but he killed her first. That poor bastard's trying to cope with the trauma of both of his best friends lying to him, and I don't envy him."

"So now we need to go and speak to Cooper. What if he was Parker? What if he was in on this all along, too?"

"Then we'll soon find out."

George took a deep breath. "We'd better nip over the road and speak to the nosy neighbour first, see if she saw anybody come here recently. Oh, and I suppose we'd better message Colin to let him know there's a body in the bungalow."

"What about getting the neighbour to call it in? Threatening her to keep her mouth shut that it was us who asked her to phone the pigs."

"Not a bad shout."

George led the way over to Maud Stokes' bungalow. She opened the door pretty quickly, which meant she'd lied to them on their previous visit that she didn't nose out of the window anymore. She had to have seen them coming.

"Yes?" She frowned at them.

George twigged she didn't have a clue who they were because of their disguises, so he introduced them.

"Would you like to come in for a cuppa?" she said. "Only I've got something to tell you. I saw someone leaving Edna's place this morning really early. He had one of those Covid face masks on which stood out to me even though it was dark. It was a white one. Anyway, it all seemed a bit suspicious, and I was contemplating whether to ring you, but here you are." She turned and walked down the hallway. "I've baked some cakes. Would you like a slice?"

George followed her into the kitchen where an array of different sponges stood in a line at the back of the worktop. "Fuck me, have you got a sweet tooth or something?"

"It's for the coffee morning at the community hall round the corner. I decided to get back out there and live life again. Oswald, he's the coffee morning organiser, will be around to pick those cakes up soon, but nobody will miss one of them. Which do you prefer?"

"Victoria Sponge," they replied at the same time.

Maud stared at them as though that had creeped her out, then she shrugged and pulled the Victoria sponge towards her. She'd dusted the top with icing sugar, jam and cream oozing out of the sides. She cut three slices and put them on small plates, then poured coffee from a full carafe. They sat at the table, and once again, she went through what she'd seen this morning.

"What else have you seen over the road lately?" George asked, then bit into his cake.

"She's been gardening a lot, but that's nothing new lately. She *has* been going out, though. I wish I could tell you where, but I haven't got a clue. Why? What's going on? What's she done?"

"Can you think back really hard to a few months ago. Did she ever have a chubby old lady visiting her?"

Maud blushed. "I didn't tell you this before because I was ashamed of what I did."

George's shoulders slumped. *For fuck's sake, what's she going to offload on us now?*

Greg paused mid-chew. "What did you do…"

"Well, I wondered who the old lady was. I thought she was staying with Edna for a while because she left early in the morning and returned in the evening. I never saw Edna during those times, only after the old woman had come home. So one night about nine, I nipped over the road as soon as the old lady went round the back of the bungalow. I went round there an' all and saw her. She had her back to me, getting undressed in the living room. She took off this suit thing, like skin. It had a big belly and fat arms. She threw it on the sofa and walked out into her hallway. I went home wondering what the hell was going on, then I told myself it was none of my business. Edna's weird enough as it is without me poking my nose in and saying something to her about it. I'd have had to admit

I'd been spying, and she'd have called the police on me."

George closed his eyes briefly to calm himself down. "So even though the last time we came here, we stressed it was important you tell us everything, and despite who we are and what we can do to people, you still chose not to say anything."

"I've been trying to turn over a new leaf and mind my own business. If I told you I hadn't done that, then it proves I'm a failure. I've always been a failure."

George wasn't interested in her self-pity, but the fact she'd fucked up went in their favour. "Now then, instead of me getting angry at you for lying to us, I want you to do something for us. Wait for a while after we've gone, then go over to Edna's and knock on the door. If anyone asks why, you're offering her an invite to go round to the community centre with you. When she doesn't answer the door, you get a bit worried and go to the back. Now listen to me—we've already been round there, and she's dead in bed." He held up a hand to stop her from protesting. "You don't actually have to nose in at her. I'll tell you exactly what she looks like so you can tell the police."

"She's *dead*?" She slapped a hand to her chest. "Oh God, why can't *you* tell them if you've already found her like that? Why does it have to be me?"

"Because you're righting a wrong. You lied to us, and now you're going to make it all better. You just do as you're told and everything will be all right."

A sly expression took over her reddened face. "Can this not wait until later this afternoon? Only, like I said, Oswald's coming for the cakes, and there's that coffee morning I want to go to. I'm going to miss out if I phone the police because they'll expect me to hang around to talk to them when they get here."

George wasn't sure he'd heard her right. "So you're prepared to leave a body on a bed so you can go out for coffee and a slice of sodding cake?"

Maud's cheeks turned redder. "It sounds bad when you say it like that, but she's dead and nothing can help her now, so a little while longer won't hurt."

George glanced at Greg. "It won't make much odds to us, will it?"

"No." Greg glared at her. "Just make sure you keep your trap shut when you're at the community centre. We're not averse to killing old ladies if we have to, so if you fuck this up, we'll come back and shut your mouth permanently."

Maud shuddered. "I think perhaps I'll do it your way after all. I can always go to next week's coffee morning."

George smiled. "Cheers. I think we'll have another slice of that cake before we go."

She cut them a big chunk each and sipped her coffee while they ate. Greg had been opposed to frightening older ladies, but it seemed he'd changed his stance on that. Maybe he'd realised it didn't matter *what* age someone was: if they were a potential problem, they needed reminding that their lives weren't that important to The Brothers.

They left her with another warning and her agreeing to go over the road after Oswald had collected the cakes. On the drive towards Kayla's block of flats, George sent Colin a warning message that someone would be phoning in about a dead body soon which could potentially be murder. Then he and Greg discussed the fact that Edna must have been *both* Ednas and Roach had likely supplied a bodysuit and disguise. Greg parked against the kerb, and they got out, taking the stairs to Kayla's floor. There was no saying whether Cooper would be in or not, but considering his girlfriend had been murdered, George reckoned he'd likely be at home. He knocked on the door and wasn't surprised to see the man opening it.

He frowned at them, and again, George remembered their disguises, letting Cooper know who they were.

"And we've come to pay our respects. And to see whether you've heard anything from her parents. We still haven't been to see them yet to offer the funeral money."

"They don't even know who I am, and I haven't bothered getting hold of them. They wouldn't want to speak to me anyway, so what's the point? Do you want a cuppa or something?"

"No, we've not long had one, but we'll come in anyway. There's something we want to ask you." George brushed past him and walked into a living room at the back. All the furniture looked new, as did the flooring. He gathered Cooper made a good living out of drugs, but so long as he paid protection money, he didn't much care what lined the bloke's pockets.

Cooper came in, followed by Greg. Cooper flopped on the sofa as though his body weighed too much and he didn't have the strength to hold it up. George sat on a swivel armchair, and Greg opted to stay by the door just in case Cooper had been involved in everything and had a mind to bolt.

"I've got to ask you some questions," George said, "but only because of a few things that have come to light. Firstly, how close were you with Kayla?"

"Close enough, but she was a bit secretive, which was something I never liked."

"What do you mean, secretive?"

"Well, when we got kicked out of the house she rented because one of the neighbours dobbed me in to the landlord for selling drugs, she didn't tell me where she'd gone to stay. I was sleeping on friends' sofas and assumed she'd gone back home to her mum and dad. But then she said she hadn't seen her parents for ages, and it got me wondering whether she had another fella on the go. We met for a drink one night in the Red Lion, and she said she'd found us a flat and the landlord was a friend of hers. She said his name was Everett, but I hadn't heard of him until then. Anyway, I didn't think much of it. We both had a past before we got together, so I shrugged it off and moved in here anyway."

"Sounds like she had something to hide then," George said.

"Seems so, because she came home from work yesterday saying someone had been watching her. I didn't know why they'd be doing that. I mean, she's just a girl who goes to work, comes home, goes to work, has a drink in the pub, know what I mean? Nothing special. Why would anyone even *be* watching her? She said it was a woman with blue hair and a man with sunglasses. She was really scared when she got in from work, worried they'd followed her in the taxi. So that's why I said for her to come to work with me last night but that I'd meet her there because I had to pick up some gear first. But then she went and got killed, so maybe she wasn't being paranoid and someone *had* been watching her after all."

"Are you saying you didn't believe her when she told you that?"

Cooper looked uncomfortable. "I feel bad, but I caught her out in a few lies sometimes. She never seemed to tell the complete truth about anything. But I still cared about her. I loved her. She must have been followed to Skein Road, but who the fuck would want to top her? What had she done before she met me for someone to hold a grudge for such a long time?"

"So you're wondering if something in her past came back to bite her on the arse?"

"Yeah, or whatever she was doing when she stayed wherever she was staying."

"Did you tell the police any of this?"

"Only that I was meeting her at the bench."

"Do you know someone called Edna?"

Cooper frowned. "I don't know many old ladies except my nan and her next-door neighbour."

"Where were you on the day that woman got shot at the hairdresser's?"

"Fucking hell, that was a while back. I can't even remember what day it was. I was probably here, dossing about."

"Did you get up and look out the front at all?"

"I don't remember what I was doing so I couldn't tell you."

"All right. Maybe this will help jog your memory. Did you see anyone get on a motorbike?"

Cooper shook his head. "It's difficult to know how to answer when I'm not even sure what I was doing that day. Sorry, but I just don't know."

George reckoned if Cooper was anything to do with Alice's murder then he'd have a nice little alibi lined up ready, which he didn't. Satisfied he was telling them the truth, he stood, ready to leave. "Is there anything else you can tell us about Kayla?"

"People wondered what I was doing going out with her. They said she was a nasty piece of work, but honestly, she was lovely to me. Whether she was a liar or not, she didn't deserve to die."

"It's looking like she did."

"What do you mean?"

"The signs are pointing to the fact that when you were sleeping on sofas, she was at a women's refuge spying on a resident. She then lured that resident to the hairdresser's so an accomplice could kill her. She used someone else's name. Called herself Vicky Hart."

Cooper shot forward to sit more upright. "What?"

"So you don't know Vicky, then? She supposedly stayed here with you for a few nights."

"No one stayed here. I might have *said* she did at some point because Kayla asked me to, but I didn't know it was to do with that murder. Fucking hell…"

"I'd be a bit more selective with who you trust in future when it comes to girlfriends, then. You've had the wool pulled well over your eyes." George walked out, shaking his head at what a blinder Kayla had played. And Precious. And that fucking Roach. Then there was Edna.

In the taxi, he said to Greg, "I think we need to speak to Boycie, see if he seems genuine or whether he slips up. It's entirely possible he didn't know a thing about this, the same as Cooper, but I'd like to look him in the eye when we ask a few questions."

Greg nodded and peeled away from the kerb. "If he's lied to us, God fucking help him."

With the Boycie chat out of the way, both of them agreeing he'd been duped by his best mates and nothing sinister was going on, the twins moved on to the next issue: Kayla's parents. They'd been let inside the house, which was a good sign, but Karen had launched an irate attack on them as soon as they'd gone into the living room.

"You're supposed to protect the residents," she screeched, "but you did nothing to save our Kayla."

"They can't be everywhere at once," James said. "You can't expect them to have eyes and ears on every part of the Estate. Kayla chose to hang around with that boyfriend of hers, and that's the only reason she's on a pathologist's table now."

"Actually," George said, "the reason she's on a pathologist's table is because she was involved in the murders that went down at the hairdresser's a few weeks ago. We haven't said anything about that to the police because we're of the understanding that you might not want your daughter's name dragged through the mud even though she's dead."

Karen stared at him, her bottom lip quivering. "What do you mean she had something to do with the hairdresser murders?"

George explained, although he didn't tell her where he'd got the information from. "But I'm telling you now, her boyfriend, Cooper, had nothing to do with this. He's a good lad and unfortunately picked the wrong girl."

Karen looked like she was about to refute that then changed her mind. "He did. Kayla was hard work, and I'm not even ashamed to say that sometimes I couldn't stand the sight of her. She's always been spiteful. I thought she'd grow out of it, but she clearly didn't."

"The police seemed to think she was killed by a druggie," James said. "I reckon it was someone she upset, but honestly, there are too many to count, but I can give you a list of who I remember if it helps. Kayla upset hell of a lot of people."

George scratched the end of his nose. "She was killed because she was a part of a murder plot. The person who murdered her didn't trust her to keep her mouth shut—and I expect you can understand why. That person has also been murdered. It's a long and complicated story which you don't need to know about." He took a thick envelope out of his suit pocket and placed it on the coffee table. "This is for the funeral. I hope it helps. I know it won't take away your grief but it *will* take away some pressure. If you think about telling the police what we've told you, we'll deny it. Then we'll send someone round here to beat the shit out of you. If you then decide to phone the police again, you'll end up dead. Sorry, but I find the truth and being blunt is best. We're sorry for your loss."

George walked out and waited for Greg in the taxi.

As they drove away, Greg laughed. "You're an unfeeling cunt sometimes."

"Yeah, well, that Karen got on my tits. She reminded me of Kayla." He sniffed. "It got the message across, and that's what counts. Shall we have some lunch at the Noodle? We need to tell Nessa that Edna's going to be a permanent no-show."

Greg nodded and drove on, letting out a long sigh.

Yeah, George felt a bit like that, too.

Chapter Twenty-Four

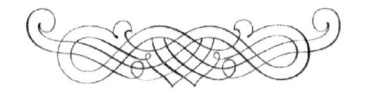

Greg didn't want to have this conversation tonight, not when he was so tired and might blurt something he'd regret—George syndrome—but he owed it to Ineke to at least explain himself. Then again, hadn't he explained himself from the beginning? But he'd be the bigger person and take the blame if it made her feel better—and to be totally honest, it would make him feel better, too.

He struggled with how he was sometimes a selfish bastard like that. The easy option of letting it fall on his shoulders saved hassle and a whopping headache. He did it a lot with George, although when it really mattered, he stood up to him. Didn't he? Not if Ineke was to be believed, he didn't. She felt he let George walk all over him, that he was his lapdog, but she just didn't understand. It had always been like that, it was safe, Greg knew where he stood. If he wanted to dig deeper, he'd acknowledge that his brother taking the reins and leading the way was a balm to his soul.

He hadn't done anything he hadn't warned Ineke about, but she wanted more than he could give her, despite agreeing that George and the Estate came first. She probably thought she could handle it, but as the days and weeks had passed, she'd likely found herself wanting more. Well, there was no likely about it, it was obvious that's what she wanted.

He pulled up outside her flat. Funny how he didn't give a shit when speaking to residents, how he could just rock up, say what he had to say, then leave. But this was different. He felt for her, he really did, but he had to get it across to her that they should never have begun a relationship in the first place. It hadn't been fair to her, nor to him, not to mention poor George. His brother acted the hardman, but the things Ineke had said hurt him, and Greg couldn't have allowed it to continue. George had always protected him no matter what, and Greg needed to do the same in return. No woman was worth upsetting George for.

He got out of their taxi and took a deep breath on the pavement. Fucking hell, what had he got himself into? No wonder neither of them bothered with women, they were either too much trouble or they just didn't get the twin bond. He couldn't expect her to, not really. She wasn't a twin herself, and while she'd grown up thinking she had a half brother, she was actually an only child. She'd been through so much, and he hadn't particularly been mindful of that.

What an arsehole.

Instead of using his key, he knocked on the door. He didn't expect her to answer, not this late, even if she *was* awake, but then she probably knew it was him and might play the game of 'let's leave him standing on the doorstep to teach him a lesson'. He sighed just at the thought of it, all the fucking about the women in his life had done. Not Mum, though, he didn't include her in that. But surprise, surprise, Ineke opened the door. She took his breath away the same as the first time he'd seen her. It must mean he had strong feelings for her, but at the same time, he had to admit this wasn't going to work.

"All right?" he asked.

"I'm better now, thank you. Did you come to collect the few bits you have here?"

"No, I came to talk."

"I think I said everything that needed to be said in the Noodle, don't you?"

"Probably, but I just wanted to make sure you were okay."

She laughed. "I suppose you thought I'd be a crying mess. If that doesn't tell me how big your ego is, I don't know what will."

Was she right? Had she made a massive point there? *Had* he expected her to be blubbering? Yes, he had. Maybe he'd hoped she'd cared about him more, that she'd want to fight for them, yet at the same time, no, he fucking well didn't. He hated being at sixes and sevens.

"I'll give you that one," he said. "I just want to say it wasn't your fault, none of it."

"I'm a big girl, I can take some of the blame. You told me from the start how it would be, and I agreed, but then I moved the goalposts. It was a bitch move, and I should never have done it. I reminded myself of my mother."

That would have burned her to admit that, and he found himself hoping she didn't harp on about it because, Jesus Christ, he didn't want to hear it. His head was too full, and her adding to it would mean he'd snap at her, something he didn't want to do. And maybe he didn't want to hear it because it would mean facing that he was an even bigger prick than he'd thought. To not want to listen to someone you cared about…that wasn't right, was it?

It was obvious she wasn't going to let him in, so he'd have to say what he had to say on the doorstep. "About your mother…"

"I know what you're going to say. I need to get my head tested. Going to see Vic for therapy clearly isn't working. I'm actually wondering whether I've have some sort of hereditary mental illness. You've only got to look at my mum to know what I'm up against."

That could have sounded like self-pity, but it came across as what he thought it was: a fact. "There might be tablets for it."

"If I'm the same as her, then yes, there are. As I told you, she chose not to take them sometimes. I wouldn't be as stupid as that." She sighed. "Look, I'm really grateful for what you, George, and Moon, did for me in Amsterdam, and I'd never, *ever* tell anyone what happened there. I'm also grateful for what you and your brother will *still* do for me by letting me live here and work for you... I won't let you down, I promise."

Had she said that because he'd got it wrong and she *was* scared of him?

"I know you won't," he said. "And I need to thank you for caring about me the way you did. Apart from my mum and George, no one's ever really given a shit." He wasn't going to go into how Mum's best friend had been like a mother to him. "Just let me know if you need anything. I'll still be here for you." A stupid bastard lump expanded in his throat. "I care about you a lot, you're just not the woman for me, and I'm not the man for you."

"I know." She smiled sadly and shut the door.

That was a bit abrupt.

How odd to want to make her open it again so he could speak to her some more. This was the right thing to do, splitting up, so why did it feel a bit wrong?

He turned and got back in the taxi, understanding George's need to become Ruffian, going out on the dark streets alone to wreak havoc. He had the burning urge inside him to hurt someone but had enough sense to drive home instead. He found George in the living room, and at the sight of his twin he felt safe enough to let the tears fall.

"Fuck me, bruv, that was hard."

George didn't get up to hug him, he knew better than to do that. "I know what you mean. Even though me and Janet weren't right for each other, it was weird for a while without her, and I'd grown to hate her, so it didn't make sense. Emotions are strange, they fuck you up. Do you want a Pot Noodle?"

Greg smiled. "Yeah, go on then."

He followed George into the kitchen and sat at the island while his brother boiled the kettle and took the pots out of the cupboard. "At the same time, I'm relieved. I can't explain it."

"I get it, it's all right."

"Thank God you get it, because I don't."

"You wait and see, things will turn out the way they're supposed to."

The backs of Greg's eyes itched. "Mum used to say that."

"And she was right. What hurts now won't hurt later, or not as much anyway."

"Do you still think about what could have been with Janet?"

George shuddered. "I try not to think about her at all, but if you mean getting married and having kids and living in our dream cottage, nah, I don't think about that anymore. It's not in my future, not while we run the Estate anyway. What are you going to do, go back to having one-night stands?"

"I'm going to give women a miss for a long while. It all does my head in." Greg got up and grabbed a couple of Cokes from the fridge. He sat back down and took in the calming effect of watching George cutting up a loaf of tiger bread. "I miss our mum."

"It hits you out of nowhere, doesn't it?"

"Yeah. She's the only woman I'll ever properly love."

"Same. She was one in a million. We'd never get that lucky to find someone like her as a wife, so why bother trying?"

"Do you reckon our standards are too high? Do we expect too much? I barely saw Ineke, didn't even give her a second thought about being home alone."

"Because she said she didn't mind and you took it at face value. It's not your fault she changed her mind. Did you say anything about her mental health?"

"I didn't have to, she said it for me. Said something about it maybe being hereditary."

"Let's hope she doesn't follow in her mum's footsteps and go weird on you like she did with Ineke's dad, all stalkery and whatever."

Greg's stomach dropped at that. "She wouldn't, would she?"

George got on with buttering the bread. "She'd better fucking not, because I'll have her if she puts one foot out of line, I've told you that before."

Greg didn't doubt it, he'd do the same for George if their situations were reversed. "Let's hope she behaves herself then, because it would be fucking odd throwing her underneath the cottage."

"Not if she pissed you off. You'd hate her then."

"I just want her to make something of herself, to be happy in her own skin."

"I think you loved her in a way. You wouldn't have said that if you didn't."

"No, I didn't love her, otherwise I'd have left running the Estate to you and spent all my time with her. The truth is, I just didn't want to, I prefer being with you, even if you are a fucking cockwomble."

George laughed and plated up the bread, placing it on the island. "You're lucky you're my brother."

"Yeah, yeah, you say that all the time. If I wasn't me, you'd beat me up for being rude, blah, blah, blah."

George's eyebrows rose. "You ought to watch yourself."

Greg smiled. "Or what?"

"I'll give you a bastard wedgie."

Greg laughed and resolved to pack his feelings away regarding Ineke. It wouldn't do him any good to dwell on it. She'd finished things, so at least she valued herself more than many other women. She was worth more than the way he'd treated her.

George brought the noodle pots over and sat. "This'll make you feel better."

Greg was transported to the past, to another kitchen, in another house, in another lifetime, where Mum was the one making the noodles. She would have known exactly what to say in this situation, but for the life of him, he couldn't think what she would have said.

"You know, Mum would tell you to buck up and stop being such a moping dickhead," George said.

It was no surprise his brother had read his thoughts. "Yeah, so maybe I'll take her advice."

"You do that, else I'll give you a clip round the earhole."

They ate their noodles, dipping the bread into the sauce. Oddly, it *did* make him feel better, even though this was George's comfort food. It was the 'same'. It was what Greg had needed for a good while. Now their lives could go back to how it had been before, and he had no one to answer to except for himself and George.

And he vowed never to get involved with a woman again if this was how they made him feel.

Chapter Twenty-Five

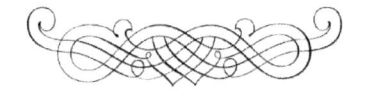

Colin got up with the lark and had chanced going around to see Janine. In her recent messages, she'd said Rosie had a habit of waking her up at four a.m. and not going back to sleep until nine. The baby liked crying during that time, and nothing Janine could do would calm her. The health visitor had said it was normal and not to worry, but of course, Janine worried. At times, she was paranoid she wasn't a good mother and never would be.

Colin pulled up outside her house and cut the engine. He walked up her front garden path and knocked quietly, realising, too late, that this might be the day that Rosie hadn't created merry hell. He'd feel bad if he'd woken the pair of them up. But a shriek from inside confirmed the little one was well and truly awake, so he knocked harder in case Janine hadn't heard him the first time.

She opened the door, and the poor cow looked knackered. She seemed relieved to see him and handed Rosie over straight away. "Take her so I can go for a wee, for God's sake."

He walked inside, and the bundle in his arms stop crying and stared up at him.

"Oh, fucking great, it's just me she doesn't like," Janine said. "She calms down for Cameron as well."

"Maybe she doesn't like women," Colin joked.

"Well, she'll just have to get used to me, won't she? I won't be a tick."

"Have a shower while you're at it," he said. "Just take a few minutes to yourself."

"I won't say no."

She went upstairs, and Colin walked into the kitchen. Rosie's eyelids drooped then closed completely. Her body relaxed, and he sat with her at the table, chuffed to bits she trusted him enough to go to sleep on him. It would probably sound stupid if he said it out loud, but he'd worried she'd know he carried badness inside him now. That was what Janine had said about herself last night in a text, that her daughter sensed her mother carried a dark passenger.

"You need to pack your behaviour in," he whispered to Rosie. "Your mum's got a heart of gold underneath it all. I don't know what I'd have done without her."

He should really stop relying on her to prop him up. Janine had enough on her plate without him turning up out of the blue. He should have messaged to make sure it was okay, too, instead of assuming she'd be able to accommodate him.

He leaned his head on the wall and closed his eyes. Having Rosie in his arms turned his inner anger down to a simmer. Maybe he should tell himself he was helping The Brothers for her benefit, making the estate a better place for her to grow up in. He tested the waters and let his mind wander to his wife and how she'd have gone all gooey at the sight of him holding a baby. Instead of crying at the thought of her, which he'd fully expected, he smiled. He couldn't remember who'd told him to do that, think of the good times rather than what had happened to her, but they'd been right.

He hadn't fallen asleep, but it felt like he had. For some reason, he seemed more rested than when he'd walked in. Perhaps that was the key to grieving, rejoicing a life well lived instead of mourning the fact she was no longer here.

He opened his eyes to find Janine staring at him.

"I can't bloody believe it," she whispered. "Can you move in and deal with her in the mornings until she's grown out of this hateful phase?"

He laughed. "I don't think Cameron would want me hanging around. Where is he anyway?"

"In bed. Rosie was a little sod all night, and he dealt with her."

"He's a good dad."

"Yep. Do you want a Pepsi Max?"

He nodded. "Is there somewhere I can put her down?"

"Hang on, I'll just get her chair." Janine left the kitchen and returned with it. She placed it on the floor. "I won't take care her off you because she'll probably sense it's me. You can pop her down."

"I don't want to drop her."

"You won't, and if you start worrying you will, she'll pick up on it and wake up. I love her to death, but believe me, I want her to stay asleep."

Colin popped the baby down, and the little bugger didn't stir. Janine watched her as if waiting for her to wake up and start screaming. She went to the fridge and took out the can for Colin, then flicked the kettle on.

"How come you're here so early?" she asked.

"I just wanted to talk about my first proper stint working for the twins, not that I've had to do anything much. There's been a murder, and Nigel's leaning towards it being drug related. That suits George and Greg, and I haven't had to steer anything in the wrong direction."

"Don't look a gift horse in the mouth. You can guarantee later down the line you're going to have a tough time at some point. Do you still think you're up to it?"

He shrugged. "Time will tell, but I'll do my best."

"Do you want to talk about it? The murder?"

While she made coffee, Colin opened his can, wincing at making a racket. He launched into the details, then asked, "Do you miss it, all this bollocks?"

"I do and I don't. The stress I can do without, but then again, I've switched one type of stress for another. That little madam pushes me to my limits, but I wouldn't be without her now. I can't even remember my life before she came along. Actually, that's a lie, I can. Being able to do what I want, when I want… I didn't appreciate it until I couldn't do it anymore." She brought her coffee over and sat. "This is going to sound weird, but it reminds me of being held captive in that flat. I've got a freedom of sorts, but not really. I'm tied to Rosie and her schedule, like I was tied to the schedule in the flat."

"Do you think you'll ever get over it?"

"No, it was too traumatic, and if you're going to ask me if you'll ever get over your wife's death, the answer is no there, too. The hurt will fade, the edges won't be so sharp, but they'll niggle you beneath the surface. Working for the twins will help. It'll give you a focus, but there will be times in the middle of the night when it all comes hurtling back. I don't know why, but since Rosie was born, I've thought about that flat a lot."

"Maybe because you have time on your hands to think. It's not like you can roll over and try to get back to sleep when you've got a baby to deal with."

"True."

"Apart from her being a little sod in the morning, is everything else okay?"

"Couldn't be better. I know I've whinged at you about being a crap mother. In all honesty, I don't think I'm doing too badly. I'm a damn sight better than my own mum, I know that much. I'd do anything for Rosie, yet all Mum did was think about herself. I can't imagine letting my child go hungry or get cold. Those things didn't bother my mother. Her main focus was getting a dick between her legs so she could feed her addiction."

"I'm sorry you had such a crap childhood, but thank God your life is so much better now."

"I feel bad that everything is going okay for me when it isn't for you."

"It's not your fault some bastard decided to rape and murder my wife."

She grimaced. "Have you spoken to the twins? Are they still at a standstill as to who it was?"

"They've got no clue, and although Nigel said he'd always keep the case open—"

"It would be open regardless because the fucker hasn't been caught."

"I know. I think what he means is he'll never stop looking. He'll work on it in between other cases."

She smiled. "So he's grown on you then?"

"You could say that." Colin got up and opened the fridge. "Shall I make breakfast for you and Cameron?"

"You don't have to do that."

"I know, but you look shattered."

He got on with making a fry-up while Janine rested her forehead on the table. It didn't take long for her to snore. Part of him wanted to tell her to go up to bed, that he'd stay here so she could get a couple of hours in, but she was so tired he'd leave her be.

She woke the moment he'd dished everything up, and Cameron appeared, his hair all over the place and his eyes red-rimmed.

"Sit your arse down," Colin said, "and eat that food before the little princess wakes up."

Cameron frowned down at his daughter. "Why is she asleep? Why isn't she screaming?"

"Because Colin's got the fucking gift, that's why," Janine said.

"He should move in with us for a bit." Cameron sat at the table and accepted the plate of breakfast and mug of tea Colin handed to him.

"That's what I said." Janine got up and collected her plate and cup before Colin could stop her.

He was tempted, not only to help them out with Rosie in the early hours but to stop himself from feeling so lonely. It would only be a plaster over the gaping wound that was his grief, though. It wouldn't fix everything. He wouldn't heal.

The scars of losing his wife would stay with him forever.

Chapter Twenty-Six

Boycie had felt the need to go to the street where he'd grown up. Maybe it was a comfort thing to return to the place where he'd once felt the safest. When he'd hit eighteen and moved out, his parents had relocated. It had been weird, he'd thought they'd stay in this street forever, always being just a walk away so he could go and be his true self for an afternoon or evening. But he couldn't expect Mum and Dad to hang around just for him, especially because he'd rarely visited. Maybe he should go to see them later. Catch the Tube and be an anonymous commuter, pretending he wasn't such a nasty fuck-up.

He stared over at the old lady's house and smiled, remembering nicking her apples. She was dead now, and he wondered whether the new people had kept the tree or cut it down. Did any of the current kids in this street steal from it, or did the children these days have more respect? Back in the day, all the kids here had been a nightmare.

Christ, the times he'd kicked a football back and forth with the other lads who'd lived here, and a few times when Roach had come round for tea. Then there was Precious, going against her parents and coming up this end, fucking about and being rude to everybody. Where had the time gone? He'd been so eager to grow up, to be rich like Roach had promised, that he belatedly realised he shouldn't have been in a rush at all.

He wandered down the street, soaking up more memories. Playing marbles at the kerb.

Pissing the girls off by jumping in when they were skipping. Splashing in puddles when someone walked by so they got wet.

The sound of a front door closing had him glancing down the road. Ginger Susie was all grown up, and it seemed she had a kid of her own. She stared over at him, frowning, then recognition dawned. She pushed a buggy up to him and smiled.

"God, I haven't seen you for years," she said. "What have you been up to?"

"This and that. You?"

She gestured to the pushchair. "Having a sprog for my sins."

He laughed—it was expected of him. "Do you still live with your mum and dad?"

"Yeah. Me and my partner are saving for a house deposit."

"Good luck with London prices."

"Oh, we don't plan to stay here. He's from Ireland, so we're going to move over there. Quiet little village."

"I was just thinking maybe I ought to bugger off. Get out of London."

"Is Precious going with you?"

"I doubt it. She's an East End girl and wouldn't want to leave." He'd have to lie like this forever when it came to her if he stuck around. He'd bump into more and more people who knew her. People who knew they were friends. How could he keep it up that she was still alive? Her parents would soon realise something was wrong when she didn't go round for her Sunday dinner every now and then.

"I must get hold of her and catch up," Susie said. "She hasn't seen my little one yet. Saying that, she never responds to my messages anyway, so I probably won't bother. She always did use me, pick me up and drop me whenever she felt like it. Still, I'm over that."

"She used me, too, so I know the feeling."

"You're best shot of her if I'm being honest. If listening to her mum is anything to go by, Precious is a law unto herself, even worse than when she was a kid. I wouldn't waste my time on her if I were you. She's always been selfish and out for what she can get, no matter who she hurts in the process."

So have I. "I know. I've been keeping my distance from her lately. Couldn't even tell you what she's up to these days."

"Right. Well, I'd best be off. I need to take this one to the childminder then get off to work."

"See you."

He watched her walk down the street. She nodded to another neighbour who came out and got in his car. Boycie didn't recognise him, so it was probably a new resident.

Staving off the urge to go and see Precious parents', he walked back to his car. Best he drove away and didn't look back. He was under no illusion that he'd have some messages coming his way soon, Precious' mum worrying about where she was and why there had been no contact. Had that Irish fella ditched her phone when he'd ditched her body? Where was she? Under the earth? In the Thames?

It was probably better that he didn't know.

He sighed and switched the engine on, thinking about letting himself into Precious' flat and collecting his things before the twins' crew turned up and cleaned it from top to bottom. They'd messaged him to say they were doing that, along with searching the place in case she'd written any notes, either on a laptop or a pad, about the Alice murder plot. Eventually, when she was reported missing by her mum and dad, the police would perhaps want to go inside, and it had to look like she'd just walked out of her life without telling anyone.

He pulled up outside the block and steeled himself to get on with it. To ignore all the memories, all the laughs they'd had there, all those meetings with Roach. Never in a million years would he have thought he'd be the last one standing out of all of them, yet here he was. He wasn't sure what he'd do with himself now, but it wouldn't be down the criminal route. Working with Roach had put him off that for life.

It was time to go on the straight and narrow.

Chapter Twenty-Seven

Goddess woke to a knock on the door. She jumped, disorientated at first, forgetting where she was. A quick glance around the room settled her nerves.

"What is it?" she asked.

"It's okay to go home now," Will said. "The two people in question are no longer an issue.

George wants us to meet them at the Noodle for breakfast. Are you okay with that?"

"Yes, that's fine. I just need to get ready."

Her room had an en suite, so she quickly hopped in the shower, surprised by how fast the twins had dealt with Farah and Joseph. For some reason she thought she'd be stuck in this house for days. But then, George *had* hinted they might take some time. Maybe it had been an easy job, but most of all, thank God she hadn't had to be involved, to see the married couple get killed. She would have done it if she'd been told to, like she'd done so many things she didn't want to, but she'd have hated it.

She got dressed, packed her few things, and they left in Will's red car. He parked at the back of the Noodle, and they walked round the front to enter the bar. The twins sat in a corner at a table for four, coffee cups in front of them, two empty. Will went to fill them up. Goddess sat opposite George and browsed the menu he handed to her. She didn't know what to say but wanted to fill the quiet. Then again, if he didn't want to speak, which she assumed he didn't because he hadn't said anything, she'd be better off keeping her mouth shut. She didn't want to piss him off.

Will returned with their drinks, then George launched into a story that was clearly about Farah and Joseph, but he disguised their names, ending by whispering about chopping off a dick and tits.

Goddess recoiled. "Oh God…" She hadn't wanted anyone to get hurt because of her, but when things were taken out of her hands, she had no control over another's actions.

"It wasn't pretty," George said, "but if people misbehave, that's the sort of reception they're going to get."

She felt sick at that but nodded and smiled, as he'd likely expect her to.

" How are you feeling, knowing they're gone?" he asked.

"Relieved, but I also feel guilty. It's my fault they're dead."

"No, it's their fault. They chose to start that business. They chose to try to force you to work there. It's all on them."

"I wonder what will happen to their house and whatever," Will said.

"Who gives a fuck?" Greg smiled. "So long as they're not living in it, what do we care? Someone went round last night and cleared out the valuables, if you catch my drift. Some of it has been stored here overnight." He nudged George.

"Oh yeah." George took a brown envelope from the inside pocket of his suit jacket and pushed it across the table to Goddess.

Paranoid someone had seen her take it and think she was a massive grass or something, she stuffed it in her handbag. "What's that for?"

"Compensation for putting up with those two pricks. Now you don't need to work at the Lantern for a while if you don't want to. There's twenty grand there. Go on holiday or something."

She almost choked at the amount. "I don't think I need one." She smiled. "Besides, Widow might not let me go. I haven't been at the Lantern long."

"If we tell her you need to go on holiday then you can go. It's fuck all to do with her. She's only running things for us. She's a front." He paused, as if he'd said too much.

She rushed in to reassure him. "I'm not about to tell anyone what you've just said. What you do is none of my business. I'm just there to earn my wages. I don't want any trouble and I never have." *Except trouble is all I'm in and I need to get out of it.*

"I expect you know the consequences if you go back on your word."

She nodded, her stomach rolling over. She really didn't want to get on their bad side; she'd thought she could do what she had to do without them even knowing she existed, but then they'd taken over the Lantern, and she couldn't think of a quicker way to get rid of Farah and Joseph than involving them.

"Do you know of anyone who needs a job, like the one Precious did?"

She hid her surprise. "Oh, is she leaving?"

"Yeah, she's already gone, so we need a greeter and flirter as soon as possible."

"I'll ask one of my friends, see if she's interested." She had one in mind who'd definitely jump at the chance, especially when it became clear that the escort agency would be closing, seeing as the owners had apparently done a runner.

They all had a fried breakfast, and afterwards, the twins dropped her home. She unpacked her things and went to one of the shoeboxes in the top of her wardrobe. She took it down and placed it on the bed, removing the lid. Stared at the burner phone inside.

She had to use it to send in the news that one of the missions was complete. Her next job was to ruin the Orange Lantern, and now she had a crush on George, she wasn't sure she wanted to. Plus, he'd made it clear what would happen to her if she went against them.

But what would happen to her if she went against the person tugging her strings? The Organiser would send someone for her, and she end up like Farah, suddenly going missing, never to be seen again. She really ought to speak to the twins about this so they could trap The Organiser who was forcing her to wreck other people's businesses. After the Orange Lantern, Goddess was supposed to move on to The Angel and then Kitchen Street, but like she'd told The Organiser, it was going to be obvious it was her if she was the one going from job to job each time a business went tits up.

The Organiser didn't care.

Goddess switched the phone on and opened the message app.

GODDESS: F AND J ARE OUT OF THE LOOP.

She pressed SEND and hated herself for it. This was going against the twins. She was supposed to tell them about anything dodgy going on; she'd made that promise when they'd spoken to everyone after taking over the Lantern. But how could she speak to them when *she* was the one being dodgy?

THE ORGANISER: DESTROY WIDOW. DO NOT CONTACT ME AGAIN UNTIL YOU HAVE.

Goddess deleted the messages and turned the phone off. This was going to be a difficult one because she liked Widow. But she liked the twins more. And she valued the life of the person she was trying to keep safe by doing this.

She sighed and popped the money George had given her in another shoebox. She had a little girl to think about. If she could save the ransom money, she'd get her back sooner.

But if I go to the twins, they might find her for me.

Unsure what to do, she put both boxes in the wardrobe and shut the door.

Then she sat and cried.

To be continued in *Redefine*,
The Cardigan Estate 34

Printed in Great Britain
by Amazon